KARMA AND OTHER STORIES

June 2007

Helen

KARMA AND OTHER STORIES

Rishi Reddi

AN ECCO BOOK

HARPER  PERENNIAL

NEW YORK • LONDON • TORONTO • SYDNEY

HARPER PERENNIAL

P.S.™ is a trademark of HarperCollins Publishers.

KARMA AND OTHER STORIES. Copyright © 2007 by Rishi Reddi. All rights reserved. Printed in the United States of America. No part of this book may be used or reproduced in any manner whatsoever without written permission except in the case of brief quotations embodied in critical articles and reviews. For information address HarperCollins Publishers, 10 East 53rd Street, New York, NY 10022.

HarperCollins books may be purchased for educational, business, or sales promotional use. For information please write: Special Markets Department, HarperCollins Publishers, 10 East 53rd Street, New York, NY 10022.

FIRST EDITION

Designed by Elliott Beard

Library of Congress Cataloging-in-Publication Data is available upon request.

ISBN: 978-0-06-089882-3
ISBN-10: 0-06-089882-8

07 08 09 10 11   ID/RRD   10 9 8 7 6 5 4 3 2 1

Alexi

CONTENTS

JUSTICE SHIVA RAM MURTHY

It is a point of discipline that Manmohan and I meet always on Thursday afternoons to take luncheon together. This is our routine now, and it began soon after my arrival in U.S. five months back: every Thursday without fail I walk from my son-in-law's home and Manu comes from his son's house and we meet in front of the old church in Copley Square. Of course for me the walking is not so hard as it is for Manu—daily I walk at least forty-five minutes for my exercise. Since I was a young man in law college in India I have been doing that and see, fifty years later I am still hale and hearty, whereas Manu is a bit lazy, has a slight paunch and experiences some difficulty climbing steps and hills and whatnot. Always he was like that, even when we were small boys. I try to tell him, but he will not listen. What to do if others do not know what is good for them?

You must know that on Christmas day, when my story begins, I had been living in U.S. for three months. Already I had opened my own bank account, obtained a law library card, and successfully settled the living arrangements with my daughter, Kirti, and her American husband. He is a good fellow, despite having only superficial knowledge of our language and traditions; it was my poor wife, who is no more, who had trouble with the marriage initially. Also I had contacted Manu, with whom I had kept in touch all these years, and we began our present custom of taking luncheon together at an Indian establishment on Boylston Street in the Back Bay area.

That Christmas day, Manu and I were to meet as usual, and every bit of the city was covered with snow and ice. I had seen snow once before, in Darjeeling in 1968, but had forgotten how one's foot will slide on it. By the luncheon hour the snow was no longer falling—still, I was surprised to see Manu wearing just a sweater and gloves, waiting for me on the park bench. Even now he does that sometimes. He thinks that he is sitting on Abid Road in Hyderabad as we used to as youngsters, watching the crowd during the hot season.

"Judge sahib, you are using a cane now, eh?" Manu called to me as I approached. Still he addresses me with the old Urdu term. Of course he tries to intimidate me by speaking English only—but it does not work. I am very very comfortable with English. All of the courts in India are operated in that language only.

"I am required to use the cane, Manu. Not out of necessity, mind you. My grandchildren gave it to me as a present for their Christmas holiday. Their feelings would be very much hurt if I left it behind."

He is a short man, much shorter than I am, so I have to look down at him anyway when we speak. But then I leaned the cane on the bench and remained standing while he sat, just so that he would know I was speaking the truth.

"Are you not cold?" I asked.

"Not at all," he said, looking casually at the old Trinity Church, making no move to get up even though some snow was blowing straight in our faces. "So you are celebrating Christmas these days, is it?"

"Are you teasing me or what, Manmohan? You know I do not like to follow these Western customs. But what else can one do when one is a foreigner in America and one's daughter has insisted on marrying a local fellow?" I picked up the cane again. "*Challo*. Are you not feeling hungry?"

"Okay, okay judge sahib." He got up from the bench and swung his arms back and forth like a monkey getting ready for exercise.

I looked at him but said nothing. Sometimes he likes to irritate me for no reason. We have many differences, Manu and I. He has lived in U.S. since he was fifty-nine years; I did not move here until I was seventy. I am very well traveled, having visited all over India, north south east west. He has been only to Bombay and Madras. I have my head full of hair, he is almost bald completely. I am a lawyer by training, he is only an engineer. Perhaps that is why I have a slightly more developed moral sense, I do not know.

I am not finding fault with Manu. We have many things in common, or we should not be friendly at all. We are the same age, we are both Murthys of the Brahmin caste, and grew up in the same neighborhood of Mozamjahi Market in the old days, when it was still a very nice neighborhood of Hyderabad. We have the misfortune to be widowers and now we both live with our respective children. We are even closely related; my father's own brother married to Manu's mother's cousin-sister. We both came from orthodox families. As boys we learned the *slokas* every day and did not take food in non-Brahmin houses, and were strict vegetarians. That is why we always like to eat our own Indian food.

"Raga Restaurant won't be open today," Manu said. "We must find somewhere else to eat."

"Why? It is a Hindu establishment after all."

"It is an *Indian* establishment, judge sahib," Manu said. "It will be closed."

"We'll see we'll see, Manu. You are not an expert on everything in America."

But when we reached the restaurant, no light was there in the building, and the chairs were turned upside down on the tables.

"As I thought," Manu said.

"Most unusual," I said, and bent forward to see if anyone was there inside. I did not want him to realize how disappointed I was. A Christmas tree was placed just beside the hostess's stand, decorated with Kashmiri ornaments. A wooden statue of Lord Ganesha stood in the window, looking back at us quite seriously, as if he too were remembering the April sun and palm trees and mango fruits of his motherland.

"*Challo*, what is there?" Manu slapped me on the back. "We will go and look for some other place."

"But why would any *other* hotel be open?"

"If you can walk just a little further in this snow, we will find another restaurant—unless you're feeling uncomfortable in the cold?"

"What are you talking? I can walk even if we go to the Himalayas and come back."

We went off and I placed my cane carefully, so as not to put it here and there if I saw some ice. But it began growing quite windy, and the snow blew from the street onto our faces, so I bent down my head and adjusted my scarf around my ears. The large toe in my left foot was paining me because of the cold. Occasionally, a car crept past on the snow-covered street, but no taxis were there at all. At last, a light showed through the window of a small eating place. A sign announced: BOYLSTON BURRITO, and underneath: MEXICAN FOOD AND FUN.

"Manmohan," I said, "let us go in here."

"But that is a fast-food type of place—you won't like it."

"Not true not true. It looks quite fine," I said, thinking only that I had lost all the sensation in my toes and then my fingers were also feeling odd. "And see—it is Mexican. It will be quite good and spicy."

"I know," Manu said. "I come here often."

Inside, a warm gust of air blew from the overhead vent. A cardboard Santa Claus, almost two meters tall, smiled at us stupidly from the corner. The floor was wet with water from the melted snow. Only a young man and a girl were sitting and eating together and another girl, about twenty-five years of age, was standing behind the counter.

Manu gave his order immediately. "Number three special."

"What is that? What is number three special?" I asked him.

"Taco salad."

"Why do you get that salad, *baba*? People here think it is vegetarian food but it is nothing but grass."

"It tastes fine to me," Manu said.

"I suppose there are beans in it?"

"It has beans, lettuce, tomato, peppers, and cheese in a bowl that is eatable. It is written there—number three special." He pointed at the menu board on the wall behind the clerk.

I did not want to tell him that I could not see the small lettering clearly. I had not visited the eye doctor, although my daughter had been insisting on it. I was getting tired of her constant worry about me. Everything in U.S. had been tiring to me in the previous few weeks—the people, the weather, the food. Thank God my wife did not have to go through this experience also. She may not have been able to adjust as well as I had been doing.

"I would like the bean-and-cheese burrito, please," I said. There was a large picture of the meal on the board with its name written underneath. It looked like a rolled-up roti.

The girl behind the counter looked at me. "I'm sorry, sir?" she asked, leaning forward. She raised her eyebrows in the strange way Americans do, which has nothing to do with being sorry at all.

"The burrito—bean-and-cheese burrito," I said.

"Don't speak so fast, judge sahib," Manu said in Hindi. "Do you think she can understand when you speak like that?"

"She should be understanding me," I replied to him, purposefully in English. "Nothing is wrong with my language."

He waved his hand in the air and turned around to select a table for us.

I looked at her. She was smiling, but not in a kindly way. "Bean-and-cheese burrito, please," I said. "With rice and Coca-Cola to drink."

"Special number four is a better deal. It'll save you some

money." She was chewing her gum very loudly, and was looking so so impatient—like a state chief minister at a village function. "And we only have Pepsi."

"Yes yes, number four then."

"What drink?" she asked.

"I said—Coca-Cola."

She handed me a cup. "You can get your *Pepsi* at the machine," she said, pointing.

I filled the cup and collected my food and sat down, putting my heavy coat and scarf on the adjacent seat. "Can you believe her arrogance?" I asked Manu. "I much prefer our Hotel Raga. They are so polite there—not at all like this rude place."

"Raga is a real restaurant, judge sahib, this is just a fast-food place. She has trouble with our Indian accent, that's all. One cannot get upset over every little thing."

"Nonsense. Everybody should be understanding English. It is the common language."

"And they don't say 'hotel' here. They say 'restaurant.' It is 'Raga Restaurant,' not 'Hotel Raga.'"

I ignored him. "Everyone in the city is so rude, actually. I do not know why Kirti's husband insists on living in the middle of this city with cars and lorries and noise noise noise everywhere. Just like the Old City neighborhoods in Hyderabad that have become so dirty. What is wrong with those nice new homes in the outskirts with the backyards and gardens and things? Everything is clean there. Then we don't have to put up with these people and walking everywhere. Mind you, I don't object to walking. The only time I drove in India was to travel back and forth from High Court to home. Otherwise, no matter where I went, it was by walking only."

Manu was cutting his salad with a knife. "But see how much freedom there is in walking," he said. "Would you learn to drive in America just to come and have lunch with me every week?"

"Why not?" I asked, swallowing my first bite. It tasted a bit unusual. How I wished I was eating that *navrattan* vegetable curry at Hotel Raga.

"It would become too inconvenient," he insisted. "Probably you would not learn how to drive at all."

I got impatient. "In the sixty-five years we have been acquainted, Manu, still you do not know me. I am a very very independent fellow. Do you remember, even when the other judges were having a driver I drove myself?" I took another bite and swallowed it without even chewing properly.

"I don't know, judge sahib. It's not easy to drive in U.S., you have to follow the rules here."

"What rules? In America there are always these rules those rules here rules there rules. They should be followed. But nobody is following them here any more than in India."

"How can you say that, judge sahib? Here people drive correctly by staying within the white lines. In India nobody pays attention to those white lines. They are just a decorative item."

I was no longer listening to him. The burrito was tasting quite funny to me, and I examined the stuffing inside. It was dark and crumbling into small pieces. I showed it to Manu, who quickly identified it as beef! He began putting some of his salad onto my plate, to share with me, claiming it was too much for him.

"Clearly I told her *bean,* Manmohan. She knew that I wanted bean!"

"It's okay, judge sahib—"

"It is not okay, Manmohan," I said. "Everything in U.S. is not just okay okay okay." I walked to the counter and held the plate out to the girl.

"What is this?"

"I'm sorry?" the girl said, raising her eyebrows again. Such a disrespectful expression.

"This—luncheon that you ordered for me—what is it?"

"That's special number four—"

"Does it have beef in it?"

"Ahhh . . . it's a beef-and-cheese burrito, yes."

"But I ordered a *bean*-and-cheese burrito."

"You told me you wanted special number four."

"No. *You* told *me* that I wanted special number four—"

"Huh?"

"Judge sahib," Manu said, catching onto my sleeve, "let's go from here. There must be some other open restaurant."

"You gave me the number four special when I told you I wanted a bean burrito," I said to the girl.

"What? Sir, I asked you whether you wanted the special because it would save you some money. If you—"

"Can you not hear correctly? I told you I wanted *bean*, not *beef*."

Manu told me later that as I pronounced these words, a little bit of saliva came from my mouth and landed on the girl's sleeve. I do not agree. I think the girl just finally realized how wrong she was. But it is true that at this point, her behavior turned quite bad, her expression became agitated, and she began to shout at me in a big voice.

"Look, if you want a refund, I'll give you your five dollars back. It's Christmas, and I don't need to be treated like this."

"Judge sahib, let's leave."

I pulled my arm out of Manu's grasp. "I don't know what you need and what you don't need, young lady. That is not my concern. But it is a basic teaching of my religion not to eat beef."

"*Challo,*" Manu said, "put on your overcoat." He was already wearing his gloves.

"Give me your name, miss," I said.

"Roxanna," she said. "Roxanna Edmond."

"And who is your manager? I would like to speak to him."

"I *am* the manager," she said, pointing to her name tag. "It says right here. Can't you read either?"

"You should be ashamed of yourself," I said. Now Manu was taking my arm and leading me away, almost by force. "You should be ashamed." I pointed the finger of my free hand at her.

"What am I supposed to be ashamed about?" she said. "Learn to be a gentleman, sir. In this country, men act like gentlemen."

I just stared at her as if I were Lord Shiva opening his third eye. How dare she say that to me, as if I didn't have a right to be here? Did she know that my only daughter had lived in Boston for fifteen years, was the wife of an American, and taught at a very prestigious college? Where else would I be staying after my wife died?

When we were alone on the sidewalk outside, Manu handed me my coat.

"Can you believe that *bevakuf* girl?" I said, patting down my hair. "What does she mean by that? In this country, men act like gentlemen?"

"Let it go, friend, let it go. She's just stupid. She doesn't know anything."

We walked together without speaking. I was so angry that for some time I did not even realize that I had water in my eyes, which were paining from the cold wind. I am glad that Manu did not notice, because maybe he would think I was weeping. Can you imagine? A former Hyderabad High Court justice crying like a small boy on the streets of Boston?

On Boylston Street we saw a car collide with a small lorry. Manu thought the accident was the lorry driver's fault and was feeling sorry for the young man who was driving the car. But I saw clearly that he had carelessly gone through the full-danger red light. That too on a snowy street when he should be driving with much caution. We stood inside the glass doors of a warm apartment building and observed as a police constable talked with the drivers and the car was towed away. I got some satisfaction from pointing out to Manu that this was yet another example of Americans not following rules. But still I could not forget that burrito girl's insult to me.

We reached my son-in-law's street about fifteen minutes later. "Manmohan, you must consult with your son and give me the name of a barrister."

"Why?"

"I am considering quite seriously of suing that restaurant."

"*Arré babré!*" He held me by the shoulder. "You are going too far. Don't lose your self-respect out of such a small thing."

Manu refuses to take a stand about some matters, even when they are quite important. He even found fault with me for protesting against the Nizam years ago, during the police action. That is where we differ, he and I. I have certain values. Sometimes I think Manu has none.

"Are you going to do it? Or shall I ask someone else?"

He kept quiet. Probably he was wondering whom else I would ask. I was wondering that too. He knew quite well that I could not ask Kirti, who would make a big fuss and inquire why I wanted to go through the work of suing someone. She thinks that I should sit calmly like a statue in her husband's living room eating *gulab jamun* and never undertaking anything unpleasant.

"I'll talk to him and let you know," Manu said without looking at me.

"When?"

"When? When?" He threw his hands up in the air. "As soon as realistically possible. But let it go, *baba*. Let it go, friend."

"That I will not do," I answered. "And I would appreciate it if you could ask him for the reference without revealing my business to him."

The snow had started falling again and the gusts were blowing as if we were standing at the highest point of Kanya Kumari and the winds from three oceans were fighting with each other. Only when we reached my son-in-law's front step did I realize what I had done. "My cane! I left it at that dirty place!" I struck my forehead with the palm of my hand. "Now I must return and collect it." Fully I intended to do so. But I could not turn to go. Did I have to meet that girl again—with her gum-chewing and her arrogant smile? I looked at Manmohan. My faithful friend closed his eyes.

"You stay here, judge sahib. I will go and get it." Then he turned and left me, shaking his head.

The next day my daughter and son-in-law took my grandsons to the science museum, because they had no school during the winter holidays. I did not feel like being at the museum with so many children screaming and shouting, so I thought it better I should stay at home. I watched a television crime drama with a young lawyer as the hero. He successfully solved the case, had an affair, and then was happy when his wife gave him a divorce. These Americans are crazy. After the program was finished, I turned off the television, sat in my favorite chair, and rang up Manu.

"Do you have the barrister's name?" I asked as soon as he picked up the telephone.

"Yes, yes," he said, sounding irritated. "My son wanted to know everything—why do I need a lawyer, what is happening, et cetera et cetera. It was not easy."

"You did not tell him, did you?"

"No. But I don't know why it's a secret."

"It is not a *secret*, Manmohan."

"Then why could I not tell him? He thought it very strange of me. My own son thought I was hiding something awful."

"Must everyone know my affairs? He is your own son, but must he know everything?"

"Don't get upset, judge sahib."

"I thought in America they respect privacy, individual rights, religion—dignity—dignity most of all."

"What does dignity have to do with it? It would be more dignified if you *didn't* sue the restaurant."

"You do not know anything about dignity, Manmohan. Tell me, would you not be feeling bad if you were in my position?"

He kept quiet for a moment. I thought maybe I had changed his mind.

"Aaaaah, now I understand," he said. "You are ashamed, is it? Yes, that's it, judge sahib. You are ashamed."

"What do you mean, *ashamed*?"

"Okay, humiliated then. You feel humiliated. But there is no need for that. These mistakes happen to all of us when we are new to the country. I know so many stories—"

"What are you talking, Manmohan? I speak English very very well, ask anyone in our community, and the beef was hidden inside the burrito, even an American could have thought it was a bean burrito only. Just give me the barrister's information. End of discussion. Case closed."

"As you wish," he sighed. "One moment. I'll get it."

Then I heard a key in the front lock and Kirti appeared at the door with my younger grandson standing behind her. He was wearing his heavy coat and his gloves, and his eyes, peeking out between his hat and muffler, were red and tired.

"Returned so quickly?"

"It's just me, Poppa," Kirti said, unzipping my grandson's coat. "I brought Vinay back because he wasn't feeling well. Scott and Chandu are still out." She led Vinay to his bedroom.

I nodded as if all was fine, but was feeling most bothered. It appeared that I was destined to have everyone know about my affairs.

Manu finally gave the barrister's information. But as I was jotting it down, Kirti returned to the room and was looking quite curiously at me.

"Okay, fine, I will call them for you," I said into the receiver, in an effort to preserve my privacy. "No problem, Manu. I will do you this favor once."

By now, Manu was quite irritated with me. "I don't know, *baba*. You do what you like and you conduct your business as you like. Sameer has already made an appointment. Second January, two o'clock." He rang off.

"No need to thank me," I said, and also hung up.

By that time, Kirti had gone to the kitchen. "Poppa, what is happening?" she called out. "Is something wrong?"

"Why? Why should something be wrong? Only thing wrong is Vinay. How is he feeling?"

"A slight fever, that's all. He's in bed and I'm warming some soup for him." She leaned her head out the kitchen door, and her long hair fell around her face in a way that reminded me of her mother. "Is Manu Uncle asking you to do something you don't want to do?"

"Nothing nothing. Just a small favor. He is my close friend, after all. Sixty-five years we have known each other."

"Since you were small boys growing up in Mozamjahi Market," she said.

"Since we were small boys growing up in Mozamjahi Market," I repeated. I closed my eyes for a moment, thinking about all that had happened since then. "Sixty-five years," I said again, and turned on the television to watch the afternoon news, but still I could sense she was looking at me as if I had done something wrong. So immediately I got up and went to her.

"I am not intimidated by living here, Kirti."

"I know, Poppa."

"I can conduct myself as a gentleman."

"Of course. You always have."

"I would appreciate it if you could make that appointment with the ophthalmologist for me," I said, returning to my favorite chair. "I would like to go for an eye exam."

One week later, after much discussion, Manu agreed to go with me to the barrister's office. He tried to say that he had no interest in coming, and that he would not be contributing to the discussion at all; I pointed out that I would give his name to the lawyer as a witness and the lawyer would be contacting him anyway. He might as well cut short the process and come in the first instance only. So, on second January, after Manu returned my cane to me and we uncharacteristically took our lunch on Friday, not Thursday, at Hotel Raga, we caught the underground train to the Financial District.

It was obvious that Manu's son-in-law had referred us to a very good firm. The office was on the twenty-first floor, and one full window, from floor to ceiling, gave a view of the harbor with its sailboats and tankers and Coast Guard motorboats. We sat on smooth black-leather chairs and watched the solicitors and barristers in their suits and ties and polished shoes. They were quite serious. They walked quickly and spoke in soft voices. The younger men looked at their elders with respect and even opened the doors for them as they came in and out. I was reminded of my own youthful days of focused discipline, arguing over the legal effect of a word or sentence, fighting for a worthy client. Definitely I approved of Manu's son's choice. Only a marble floor was needed. They had only the wooden type that these locals like so much.

Manu was sitting in his chair like a small boy in the school principal's office. Sometimes he bent to one side, sometimes he bent to the other, then he would not look at anyone or anything in the room, then he checked his watch, as if he did not want to be there at all. It was very irritating to me, as I was under tension. He told me to stop tapping my cane on the floor, as if *I* was irritating to *him*! It was our good fortune that we waited only a few minutes when a young girl greeted us.

"Mr. Murthy, and Mr.—"

"Yes, I am Justice Shiva Ram Murthy," I said, standing. "I have the appointment today. This is Mr. Murali Manmohan Murthy."

"I'm Sarah, Kelly Golden's assistant. Nice to meet you both. Please follow me," she said. We had waited only ten minutes. That made me think that Kelly Golden could not be a good attorney, though he worked in a posh firm. If truly he was well respected, he should have kept us sitting at least thirty minutes.

We walked down a long corridor and turned into an office. A woman sat behind the desk and stood up as we entered. "Hello," she said, shaking my hand. "I'm Kelly Golden. Sorry to be a little late. Good to meet you— Mr. Murthy?"

I was confused. But only for a moment. After all, I am a modern-thinking man, and there are lady lawyers in India also. "I am Justice Shiva Ram Murthy. This is Mr. Murali Manmohan Murthy," I said calmly.

"Sameer's father—how very nice to meet you." She smiled most graciously. "I have known Sameer for years. Please, have a seat." We sat down in the comfortable upholstered chairs. To my right, Kelly Golden's window opened to the same view of Boston Harbor that we enjoyed in the waiting room. Perhaps she was well respected, after all.

"How interesting, you are a judge," she said to me.

"I retired ten years ago. For twenty-two years I sat on the Hyderabad High Court back home in India. Before that I had my own practice."

"You must miss working in the law." Her gleaming brown hair reflected the sunlight nicely, and I thought her eyes were quite remarkable.

"I very much miss the intellectual challenge," I said.

"When did you move to Boston?"

"Only three months back. But you see, I would not have left Hyderabad at all if my daughter did not need my assistance here." Manu looked at me, but I ignored him.

"I'm sure she's very appreciative," Kelly Golden said.

"It is our Indian way. Family is most important."

"I learned a lot about Indian culture from Sameer, you know," she said, addressing Manu. "We were at MIT together. He'd tell us about you and his mother and life as a boy in India."

Manu waved his hand in the air and smiled a bit shyly. "I hope he did not bore you too much."

"It was fascinating. He talked about Hyderabad all the time. He used to help me study for our physics exams." She smiled. Even though she must have been forty years, she was a pretty girl.

"Oh, he's always willing to help if he thinks someone knows less than him," Manu said lightly. "In my case, Sameer thinks that a lot."

Kelly Golden caught the joke and laughed. "But for me, Sameer's help was *truly* needed," she said.

"I doubt that," Manu said. "Probably he just wanted to talk with a good-looking classmate."

"And I see where he gets his charm from!"

Now Manu laughed too.

What was all this laughing laughing? Didn't we have some serious business to discuss without Manu acting inappropriately with a woman much younger to him? I tapped my cane against the floor and waited for them to stop their silliness.

"Please give my best to him and Priya," Kelly Golden said to

Manu before turning back to me. "Now, Sameer said that you both had something to talk with me about." She took a pen and paper pad out of her desk drawer and placed them in front of her. "I suggested to him that we could talk on the phone—"

"No no," I said. "Very much I wanted to come and discuss matters with you in person."

"What can I help you with?"

I breathed in deeply, breathed out, then explained my custom of taking lunch with Manu every Thursday. "But last Thursday it was the Christmas holiday and the Indian establishment that we patronize was closed. We were forced to eat at a Mexican fast-food establishment."

"I'm quite familiar with the situation," Kelly Golden said. "I'm Jewish, so I'm often looking for something to do on Christmas day myself. For my family, it's usually Chinese takeout and a movie."

"Then you must be knowing how I felt that day!" I leaned forward in my chair and told her about special number four, and how the girl manager had rudely put forward an order of beef-and-cheese burrito, even after I had requested a bean-and-cheese burrito. Manu was being very quiet. "You thought the girl manager was very arrogant, also, isn't it, Manmohan?" I asked.

Manu cleared his throat and addressed Kelly Golden. "I wasn't there, that's the problem—I was already sitting down to eat my food."

"But you could *see* her," I asked, "that expression on her face, correct?"

Manu turned towards me, blinked his eyes, and said nothing. I looked back at him, waiting. He was incredible. First, he made an appointment with a lady lawyer, then he was flirting with her like a Westerner, then he was refusing to support me in my position. I was about to address him with an appropriate Urdu curse when Kelly Golden spoke.

"Why don't you tell me exactly what happened after you ordered?" she said, picking up her pen.

I gave a deep sigh and closed my eyes and cleared my thoughts of the traitor who was sitting next to me. A disciplined mind is quite capable of doing these things. Then I told, from A to Zed, exactly what happened on Christmas. When I completed the story I put a piece of paper with Roxanna Edmond's name in front of Kelly Golden.

She did not look at it. She stopped writing on the notepad. "You don't eat beef," she said.

"It is against the customs of my faith to eat beef," I said.

"I'm aware of that."

"I have never, never, eaten beef in my life, before this incident. It has never passed my lips. I am a Brahmin, you see."

"It's true," Manu said, "he has never eaten beef as far as I know."

I glanced at him from the corner of my eye. Why was he talking now?

"Not only beef," I said, ignoring him. "I am completely vegetarian. No meat of any kind, or eggs. It is the doctrine of Ahimsa. Nonviolence towards any living thing. Even he is the same." I pointed at Manu with my chin.

"What happened to you after the visit to the restaurant?" she asked. "Any perceivable effects?"

"Perceivable effects?" I said.

"You might have had an emotional reaction. Did you have increased conflict at home? Any strained relationships? Any outward signs of distress?"

"I live with my daughter and my son-in-law. But I did not tell them about it."

She leaned back in her chair and looked at me for a moment. "What were you hoping to have happen in this case, Justice Murthy?"

"I am thinking to sue the restaurant, of course."

She nodded her head slowly, but said nothing. Did she have no sympathy for my position?

"I can understand how you feel, but I don't think we would have a successful lawsuit in this situation. The law requires that there be some tangible, perceivable effects of the wrong you suffered. *I* can see that you were quite upset and harmed by the incident. Your friend can see that you were quite upset. But the law won't recognize it. I would suggest, instead, that you write a letter of formal complaint to the owner and the franchise. It's quite probable that the manager would be disciplined. That would address the real issue as well, the rudeness and insensitivity of this particular employee."

"You will not bring the case?" I said, not quite believing her.

"It would be frivolous to bring suit. Surely you would think so if you were sitting in judgment on this case under Massachusetts law."

I shook my head. "This. Is. An. Important. Hindu. Practice." I tapped the floor with my cane at each word.

Manu put his hand on my arm. "Don't become so angry, judge sahib," he said.

"I suppose *you* don't follow any dietary laws?" I said to Kelly Golden. "You are not a religious person?"

She raised her eyebrows, just like the girl at the fast-food counter. "I'm not sure what my habits have to do with the situation, Mr. Murthy." Her face turned a bit red.

"*Justice* Murthy," I corrected.

"Justice Murthy. Under our legal system, there must be some definite suffering of an emotional or physical type. We could file the case, but it would get thrown out. I might even get sanctioned. Merely eating a kind of meat because of a cashier's carelessness will not get you any money."

I gazed through the window at the harbor. In the cold glare of the Boston sun, my old life disappeared: the dark chambers of the Hyderabad High Court; my wife sitting in the shade of our banyan tree; myself as a young man, holding baby Kirti's hand as we walk to the vegetable stand behind our home. Shadows in a seventy-year-old mind.

"Definitely this is not about money," I muttered, closing my eyes. "It is the principle of it all." There was nothing more to be said. Kelly Golden and myself could not understand each other. I was standing up to take my leave, but because I am a polite man—a gentleman—I said, "Thank you for meeting with me today." Manu said good-bye and followed behind me.

In the lift I could not speak to him.

"Sorry, judge sahib."

I kept quiet.

"From the beginning, I did not feel that it was the correct thing to do."

Again, I said nothing.

"*Arré*, I tried to tell you, didn't I?" he said more loudly. "I tried to say that I did not want to be involved?"

"You are a traitor. And you are no better than those people, that burrito girl and the lady lawyer. Don't walk with me, traitor, from now on I have no association with you." Quickly I crossed the lobby and stepped outside to the street. He followed.

"Even if *I* agreed with you, *she* didn't think you had a case."

"Any barrister with some thinking power could make a case," I shouted back. "All I must do is find an intelligent lawyer."

"Shiva Ram!" Manu said, catching up to me.

"Not to worry. I have no need of your help. I see what type of help you give. If a mere clerk insults your religious customs, you do not care. If she tells your lifelong friend that he does not belong in this country, it is no concern of yours."

He caught hold of my arm and stopped me. "Be a little reasonable! You can't teach her a lesson by suing the restaurant about her mistake."

"You are a coward."

His face grew red and his eyes were as wide as a *sapota* fruit. "And you are a big daring fellow. That is why you go insulting ladies who don't agree with you."

"My whole life I have felt that you are a coward. Now finally I am saying it. You have never had the courage to follow your own beliefs. Even when we were boys you were always following following whatever I did, feeling jealous of me."

"That's what you think, is it?"

"Yes."

"All of these years that is how you have regarded our friendship?"

"Without question."

"Then let me tell you, Shiva Ram, that I have been eating meat for years. Not just meat, but beef, since the second day that I came to this country. I haven't told you because it would have disturbed you too much. Now what do you say?"

Silently I stared at him: his bald, coconut-shaped head, his skin, two shades lighter than it was during our youth in the Indian sun, the lines that had spread themselves around his eyes and mouth. At that moment, no one was there in the world that I hated more. I felt like giving a slap to him, right there on his face. But I could not degrade myself in that way. "You are an idiot," I said, and walked off. He did not follow me, thank God, because I might have been forced into some action that later I would have regretted.

After some days, while I was still searching for a competent barrister, I wrote a very strong letter to the proprietor of Boylston Burrito hotel. He took full seven weeks to respond, and I was thinking he must be a typically rude American. Finally he sent a reply saying that he was quite sorry about the incident and had taken care of the manager's attitude and put her in her place. The letter was so obliging, so polite, I thought perhaps there are some good people living in U.S. after all.

I took great pains to give a proper and dignified response. For nine, ten days I thought about the matter and drafted many versions of my reply. Only yesterday morning I decided— better that I should follow the gracious route. *Considering the appropriate actions you have taken,* I wrote to the proprietor, *the event has been forgiven and forgotten. Please do not worry. I will not be bringing a lawsuit against you or your establishment.* Even in the old days, my fellow judges criticized me for being too compassionate.

Just this afternoon I sent off the letter. As I walked to the post office, I noticed the first green buds are on the trees. The snow is melting melting so fast a small river is flowing on the side of every road, just like during the monsoon back at home. The local people on the streets are greeting each other and smiling again.

One final matter. Three weeks after the Kelly Golden meeting, I felt sorry for Manu and rang up to invite him to take luncheon with me. Of course, he did not apologize, but we went to Hotel Raga and ate *navrattan* vegetable curry and *palak paneer*, and my favorite waiter served us quite nicely. America is a lonely place, after all, and I did not wish to isolate Manu without any friends, without anyone to understand him and keep him company, no matter how much he had given up our customs. We Indians must stick together.

LAKSHMI AND THE LIBRARIAN

Lakshmi Chundi, first-generation Indian immigrant, forty-seven-year-old homemaker, wife of a gainfully employed computer-software engineer working at a reputable computer-manufacturing corporation, mother of two grown sons, is melancholy. She knows why she is so. It is not only because her youngest son left for college two months ago, not only because her husband has doubled the number of his card nights since then, not only because she feels uncomfortable with her eldest son's new wife; it is also because when she went to the Lexington public library last night, Elias Filian, the town librarian, was sad.

She knew immediately when she stood at the circulation desk and his eyes barely met hers, his hands shaking as he passed her book through the sensor light. There was no exchange of the usual pleasantries. No chatting about the last book she read. A full day later, this disturbs Lakshmi very much.

"What are you thinking about? Lakshmi?" Venkat calls to her as she puts the dinner plates in the dishwasher. He is wearing his jacket, and his car keys jingle from inside the pocket.

"You are going?" Lakshmi asks in Telugu, using the polite form of address that is proper for a wife to use. She cannot remember ever having called him by his first name.

"You haven't been hearing me then?" He taps his ear with his finger. "I am going to Gopal's. To win back the money I lost last week. Lock the doors and keep safe." Lakshmi cringes when she hears these words. There is no reason for such caution in this very safe, middle-class suburb of Boston.

She pictures the scene in Gopal's basement: ten or twelve grown men sitting cross-legged on a bedsheet laid out on the floor. Each with a glass of whiskey and a pile of folded bills.

"It is warm tonight, maybe I will go for a walk." Her manner is uncharacteristically determined.

He raises his bushy eyebrows. Lakshmi knows that he does not like the thought that someone from the Indian community might see her on the street late at night. What would people think?

"Don't stay out past eight-thirty, or nine. It won't be safe to walk home."

When the door closes behind him, she goes to the back porch and looks up at the October sky. There is nothing to do inside the house except read the book she checked out from the library last night. She has never enjoyed watching American TV; she does not approve of the dating and free sex that is often on the shows. Not many programs support the Indian ideals of family: marriages that remain intact over decades, children who respect and obey parents.

She sighs and sits on a patio chair, lifting her sari high enough so that the cool autumn air can soothe her legs. She has a few friends in and near Lexington, but they are really wives of Venkat's friends: Amruta, Vijaya, Rukmini. Venkat will see all of their husbands tonight.

When she was a younger woman, she thought she enjoyed their friendship. She used to wish that her Sridher, after graduating from medical school, would marry Amruta's eldest daughter. But in the end, he was happy when his marriage was settled with a medical graduate from India. Lakshmi's own brother had found the girl.

She should be happy, she tells herself. What Indian mother wouldn't be happy with a son who was so comfortable with the traditional way? But like a nagging tug in her mind, she also feels a vague sense of disappointment. Didn't Sridher want more for himself—something of the greatness of life, the vastness of it? She felt this vastness once, when she was young and had a handsome husband with wild plans to come to the United States. Then, she thought of herself as one of the heroines of the cinemas she loved or the romance novels she read as a teenager.

But Sridher was like his father, who believed movies and books were trivial occupations compared to the strength and firmness of numbers. And wasn't it true that Venkat's skill with math, his occupation as a computer engineer, put food on the table? So Lakshmi did what every good wife should do. She adjusted herself to her husband's whims and refrained from challenging him.

Lakshmi stands abruptly. The chair almost topples behind her. What good are thoughts like these? The library is open late tonight; she will walk there and find out why Mr. Filian is feeling so sad.

The first time that Lakshmi Chundi met Elias Filian was when she brought Sridher and Sharath, then young boys, to the newly renovated public library in Lexington. She remembers that evening, only two weeks after moving into their new house. Venkat had departed to play rummy, and she was dismayed that he would come back at dawn smelling of spirits, a few hundred dollars poorer, when all she would have done was put the boys to bed and fallen asleep.

It was mid-May and the huge oak tree in the front yard had just budded tender green leaves. The mild air carried a faint scent of honeysuckle, reminding her of the jasmine-laced breezes of her youth. She set out for a walk with enthusiasm for her new neighborhood, two adoring children, and a belief that her life would provide some excitement. She was only thirty-one years old.

Elias M. Filian, chief librarian of the Cary Memorial Public Library, had been promoted to that post only a week earlier. This day, he saw a young woman dressed in a cream cotton sari, leading a small boy by each hand, standing on the new lawn in front of the library. Only that morning he had to shoo four people off the grass, one of them a burly six-foot construction worker. How discourteous they had been to him! How incon-siderate! He thought about the young shoots striving to make it up through the protective hay and, as graceful and light-footed as this lady no doubt was, he could not resist the urge to march out of the building to the front walk and inform her, quite in-sistently, of her transgression.

"Young lady!" he called, although she was not more than a year younger than he. "Madam!"

She looked up to find a peculiar, slender man wearing suspenders and bow tie, striding fiercely toward her.

"What is the matter?" she said, alarmed. Elias Filian reflected that the four people this morning had required a full explanation of their violations, and even then they were unrepentant.

"Look! Just look at what you are doing! This new grass needs care to grow. Look at how you're trampling—"

"Oh! So sorry!" She immediately hopped off the lawn in two steps, the *pallu* of her sari trailing behind her. "I didn't notice that it was young grass—but yes, there is the little bit of hay there." She was a new neighbor, and it wouldn't do to anger the locals. "Please excuse me."

Elias Filian, unaccustomed to being taken seriously, peered down into the young woman's face with something akin to disbelief. But her lovely, dark, almond-shaped eyes, framed artistically with a slender line of kohl, gazed sincerely back at him. He noticed the way her hair, cut to an attractive length, just grazed her collarbone, visible above the neckline of her sari. Suddenly, his anger fizzled to nothing. "It is quite all right, madam," he said, surprising even himself. "Nothing that the grass can't survive."

"Is this the library?"

"It is indeed. May I introduce myself." He bowed ever so slightly and said, "Elias M. Filian, chief librarian, at your service."

Lakshmi blushed, more because the young man had extended his right hand than because of intensity of feeling, and she did not feel comfortable shaking it. She quickly introduced

Sridher and, under the guise of teaching some manners, implored him to shake the librarian's hand. Then she introduced Sharath.

"I was hoping to show them the library and make them to get interested in books."

"Ah! Let us go inside. I will show you the children's section." He opened the front door, allowed her to step inside first, and led her to the spacious reception area. They walked through all the bookshelves in the juvenile department, as well as the reference tools. Lakshmi seemed so genuinely interested in the entire library that, by the end of the afternoon, he had shown her each floor and given her a small lesson in the Dewey decimal system as well. Lakshmi noted that he called her "madam" or "Mrs. Chundi" during the entire tour. For some reason, this pleased her very much.

Mr. Filian went home that night, fed his eight cats, trimmed his bonsai tree, and wrote in his journal about this young woman's eyes and her black hair and her collarbone, and her cream-colored sari, and the charming way in which she held a small son by each hand.

But their friendship had not developed beyond that level of politeness. Mr. Filian's formal manners, peculiar for suburban America, served the relationship well. Lakshmi Chundi was comfortable with him, and he took no liberties with her. His eyes did not linger too long on her face when they spoke; he lowered them respectfully during any lengthy discussion. He took great pains always to help her sons with a research project, and, because he had met Venkat one evening when he called for them at the library, Elias Filian would always ask about her husband in a most polite way.

Mr. Filian did not leave the circulation desk to help anyone other than Mrs. Chundi find books or do research; he usually asked one of the junior librarians to do that. The other librarians noted his attentions and at first gossiped about it with great interest. But when it did not seem that Mrs. Chundi and Mr. Filian ever met surreptitiously for lunch, or whispered secretively on the telephone, or spoke about anything of a personal nature at all, the other librarians' interest waned. They became accustomed to seeing Mr. Filian giving Mrs. Chundi special consideration, perhaps because she did not speak English as well as the other Indians. She needed additional help, or so they thought. They had long noted that Mr. Filian had no romantic interest in anyone, not even a secret infatuation with another man. As the years went by, and his hair turned from brown to salt-and-pepper, then finally to gray, they ceased to wonder at all about the attention Mr. Filian continued to give to this lady.

On this October evening fifteen years later, Lakshmi comes into the warm library from the brisk autumn air outside. Mr. Filian is standing behind the circulation desk. He is not looking well. Dark circles frame his eyes, and Lakshmi thinks that his slim body appears gaunt and listless.

As she walks toward the desk, she is caught in a panic. She does not know why she has come, or what she should say to him. Mr. Filian knows that Lakshmi reads only one book at a time. She takes a long time to read English text—she had come only yesterday for a book, and he would know that she is lying if she tells him she is finished.

Lakshmi leans over the counter, looks surreptitiously over her shoulder, and whispers, "Mr. Filian, my husband needs a book."

"I was wondering why you were here again so soon, Mrs. Chundi."

"You know how he feels about libraries, Mr. Filian. It was enough work for him to just pick up the boys here when they were young. Now he is going on a business trip to Japan and needs to know something about their customs. He wouldn't let me spend any money at a bookstore, so I am here." She is still speaking in a whisper, and when she realizes she is leaning toward him in a suspicious manner, she straightens herself and modestly adjusts her sari around her shoulders.

"It isn't very busy tonight, Mrs. Chundi, I can step away from the desk and show you where to find it." He turns to his assistant. "Mrs. Stern, Mrs. Chundi and I are going upstairs, could you see to the desk for a while?" Lucia Stern nods primly, without looking at them. Lakshmi thinks Mr. Filian's voice is uncharacteristically hoarse and feeble; she wonders if he has a bad cold. Could that be the reason for his listlessness?

She follows him as he walks slowly toward the stairs to the second-floor travel section. "Are you enjoying that book you took out yesterday?" His shoulders droop as he looks down at her. "What was it, *In Search of the Cradle of Civilization*?"

Despite her surprise at his appearance, Lakshmi notes with satisfaction that, as usual, Mr. Filian remembers the book he checked out for her. "The first chapter was quite interesting, Mr. Filian, quite interesting. It seems there is a theory that the ancient Aryans came from what is now central Turkey, not from Europe, as was commonly thought before. They migrated from Turkey to India and to other parts of Europe."

Mr. Filian's eyes dart around without focus, as if he has taken too much cold medicine, thinks Lakshmi.

"What evidence have they found?" he asks finally. "Is it convincing?" His hand shakes as he reaches for the stair rail.

"Of course the authors are quite convinced of their correctness. An Indian could be quite proud if what they say is true."

"No doubt, Mrs. Chundi, no doubt." Mr. Filian grips the handrail carefully. At the top of the stairs, his foot snags the carpet; he trips and catches himself with great effort. Lakshmi stifles a cry.

"Mr. Filian, I must ask you something," she says, after they collect themselves.

"Yes?"

"We have been friends for a very long time, isn't it? We have known each other for a full fifteen years?"

"I do believe so, Mrs. Chundi."

"I must ask you, and hope you don't think me too bold—but you are not looking well—and I must ask if you are in bad health or if something is wrong. Please forgive my rudeness, but I feel I would be betraying our friendship if I did not ask."

There is no doubt that Elias Filian is shocked; he tries to clear the frog in his throat. He shifts his weight from one foot to the other.

"I'm touched by what you call your rudeness, Mrs. Chundi. Indeed, you're the only one who has noticed at all." He reaches inside his pocket and removes his handkerchief, holding it to his eyes for a moment too long. Lakshmi ventures, ever so timidly, to lay her slender hand on his arm.

He lets out a small sob. "My mother is dying," he says in a hoarse whisper. "And I have not seen her in ten years. We quarreled—"

Lakshmi Chundi's hand flies to her mouth. She bites down

on her fist and, though she is not a religious woman, exclaims, "*Hai, Ram!*" She does not know if she is more shocked that Mr. Filian's mother is gravely ill or that he has not seen her in a decade.

"Sit down, sit down, Mr. Filian." She directs him to a chair. "I had no idea that this was the news. But look at you, I fear you are ill yourself."

The pair remains in the reading room of the library for more than an hour. Mr. Filian is collapsed in his chair, telling Mrs. Chundi about what he has heard from his mother's doctor over the telephone. She is in a hospital in Nashua, New Hampshire, diagnosed with cancer. She does not have long to live. She is in pain, but she has not asked for him. He is the only living relative his mother has, other than a great-niece who lives in Rhode Island. Mr. Filian's father died long ago, before he even moved to Massachusetts.

Lakshmi feels more comfortable with Mr. Filian than she ever has before. She listens to his story with patience. She pats his hand at the appropriate times. She feels the tears gather and dabs her eyes with the end of her sari. At eight forty-five, Lucia comes upstairs to tell them that the library is closing. Lakshmi leaves Mr. Filian reluctantly, telling him to be strong, everything happens for a reason. She steps into the chilly autumn air with a heavy feeling in her heart. She shakes her head in disbelief. How much trouble these Americans have with family ties!

The next morning, Lakshmi is up and dressed early, even though it is Saturday. She is going to Amruta's house to help with preparations for the annual dinner and dance recital to celebrate Diwali. She is looking forward to some time with companions outside her home. When she leaves the house at nine, Venkat is sitting in the den in his robe, watching the previews for a tennis tournament.

The air is cool, and a bright autumn sun cheers her on the short drive to Amruta's house. Amruta is a classical *bharatha natyam* dance instructor and the cultural director for the Telugu Association of Eastern Massachusetts. Lakshmi parks in the circular drive to the large brick home and enters through the garage door without knocking. Although Amruta's husband owns a very lucrative computer software business, Lakshmi never feels that Amruta tries to show off her money.

Amruta, Vijaya, and Rukmini are sitting in the family room in the basement, surrounded by tambourines, poster board, and packages filled with cotton balls, which will be used to make small cotton wicks for the oil lamps. A song from a popular new Hindi film plays in the background. The women are laughing and chattering. Rukmini's round face looks up when Lakshmi enters.

"We will ask Lakshmi Auntie then!" Rukmini exclaims, as if Lakshmi has been in their conversation from the beginning. Rukmini is the youngest of the group. Although she calls all of the middle-aged women "auntie," only Amruta is Rukmini's aunt by blood.

"Go ahead, she will only agree with me," Amruta challenges her. Amruta's hair is pulled away from her dark face and tied in a knot at the nape of her neck. She is wearing a plain cotton sari and seems ready to work.

"Auntie"—Rukmini turns to Lakshmi—"what was the first year Lata Mangeshker appeared in the *Guinness Book of World*

Records for having the most recordings?" Rukmini's face is slightly red and full of excitement. She has drawn her *bindi* a bit bigger than usual today, and it accentuates the wide space between her eyes, the innocence conveyed in her features. Lakshmi wonders how this young wife and mother manages to become excited about the most mundane things.

"That I don't know. Nineteen seventy-one maybe? Later than that?" Lakshmi smiles at her. She takes off her shoes, gathers her sari around her, and sits on the floor between several pieces of cardboard.

"Auntie, you are totally wrong." Rukmini pouts while Amruta chuckles quietly.

"What did I tell you? It is definitely not before nineteen seventy."

"All of you are wrong," cuts in Vijaya. "Lata Mangeshker earned that record even before nineteen sixty-five. After I go home and check the book I will let you know the exact date." Vijaya's face is set in the grim way of those who are not usually challenged. Her sharp nose, her glasses, and the contrast between her very fair skin and jet-black hair only compound this impression.

"Then let us put off the subject for another day," suggests Lakshmi.

When the four women are settled in the family room, Amruta explains what needs to be done: signs announcing the location of the event, cooking assignments, clean-up duty. But the most tedious task is making a hundred *deepam* wicks by cutting the cotton into small pieces and rolling them, in the old-fashioned style, to place in tiny steel oil-filled bowls that will line the perimeter of the stage.

"Such a ridiculous idea this is!" Vijaya says. She is sitting on the floor cross-legged and straightens her back slowly. It is late morning, and the plate is only half-full. "Next year we must object to this idea. White Christmas lights will do just as well. It is that Harish Rao on the Directors Board. 'Tradition,' he says! Always he is willing to make more work for others."

"What time did the rummy game end last night?" asks Lakshmi. "I am sure that Harish Rao was here until the very end."

"It is terrible how late these men stay for rummy," says Vijaya.

"Sometimes you think they care more about the game than about us," Rukmini adds, but she is smiling.

"You joke, Rukmini, but sometimes I think it is true."

Lakshmi says nothing.

"I don't think we will finish today," says Amruta. "We should set another day to complete the tambourines and the signs."

"Thursday, after lunch," suggests Vijaya. The women agree.

"And where is Shailaja?" Lakshmi asks. "Things would finish much faster if she were here."

"She phoned this morning and said that she wasn't feeling well," Amruta answers. "It doesn't surprise me. Even her husband was so sick last night. But still he came to play rummy."

"Everybody is having colds now," Rukmini says. "In Ram's school half the kindergarten class is sick. I am scared to even send him there Monday, poor little thing."

Lakshmi notes the sweetness in Rukmini's voice. Was she that caring when she was a young mother? She wonders when she changed. Was it when Sridher moved to Chicago for that residency program, not worried that his parents were a thousand miles away? Was it when Sharath went to college and stopped calling?

"She has more than one reason to be feeling ill," volunteers Vijaya mysteriously.

"Why?"

"Didn't you know?" Vijaya is silent for a moment, pausing for effect. "Her daughter Lata is having a love affair, and she came right out and told her parents. No shame at all."

The women gasp.

"Don't be surprised. She is that type anyway. She was coming out of the cinema with a boy when I saw her—holding hands. When she saw me, she pulled her hand away and tried to act innocent. But I know. I saw." Vijaya points to her eyes.

"Was he one of our boys?" asks Lakshmi.

"He had blond hair and an earring. You tell me if he was one of our boys! He had those torn jeans also. I don't understand what sort of fashion is that?"

"Do you think Shailaja knows?"

"Of course she knows. Would I be a good friend if I didn't tell her? But it seems that her daughter had already admitted it to her a few days before. If anyone sees my Anjuli doing that sort of thing, I would expect them to tell me," puffs Vijaya. "Of course, I doubt that anything of the sort would happen to Anjuli. She seems to have a very level head on her shoulders."

Lakshmi remembers when Sridher was sixteen years old. Long ago, she thought that her boys were always good and that they were never tempted to date American girls. But what did she really know about her sons? Didn't Sridher always have a mind of his own? And who knows what Sharath is doing in college? Suddenly she is annoyed. "We never suspect what our children will do, Vijaya. We think we know them, but we don't. We don't know them at all."

Vijaya scowls. "Maybe sons are like that, but definitely daughters are not. Everybody says they want sons sons sons, but in the end, it is daughters who remain close to you and take care of you and are honest. You might not be knowing that, Lakshmi, with your two boys."

Rukmini's wide eyes dart between them. "It is hard with girls, I think," she says, trying to draw a truce. "Of course I don't know, but I think that parents worry about a daughter so much more." Amruta glances at her with appreciation.

"Look at me," Amruta says lightly, "I was worrying so much about finding a match for Supriya. Thank God we found Sameer. It is difficult for these Indian girls who grow up here, they become too sophisticated. 'We want a liberal guy, Mom'"—Amruta crosses her legs and mimics an exaggerated American accent—"'he has to help with the housework and raising the kids and be supportive in my career.'" She shakes her head. "I say, first pass your exams so that you have a career before you make those demands." The women, except for Lakshmi, laugh at this.

"They are so different from us, you know," Amruta continues. "All we knew before we were married was going to Hindi cinemas with our friends and listening to what our parents told us. These girls today, they expect too much. I just wanted a boy with a good education from a good family."

"What more can you ask, really?" adds Vijaya.

For a moment, Lakshmi remembers a night twenty-six years ago. Venkat had just finished a posting in a small village outside of Hyderabad. She was living with her parents until his return. She had not seen her new husband in a month. He came back that night, riding his motorcycle, smelling fresh and clean and strong. So like a man, she thought. Her husband. He brought her a strand of white jasmine and pinned it in her hair with his own fingers. They went to a movie that night, *Bis Saal Baad*; the title meant "Twenty Years Later." It was already an old movie then, in haunting black and white. The night was magical; she does not know whether it was because she loved the movie, or because she loved her husband, who had returned to her. She remembers climbing behind Venkat on the motorcycle, the moonlight reflecting from its chrome body, and tightly gripping her husband's waist. Her sari swept out gracefully behind them as the motorcycle began to move. She turned to wave at her little sister, Radha, standing on the veranda. Radha waved back playfully, laughing and calling out to them . . .

"You were really lucky too, Lakshmi," says Amruta. "Sridher was so cooperative and mature. He just went to India and liked the girl you picked. You can see just by looking at her: a nice girl from a nice family. She is pretty and also a doctor. Really you are lucky."

"Yes," Lakshmi agrees, without enthusiasm. "She is good. A nice girl."

The women cluck in agreement.

The next morning, after Venkat leaves for work, Lakshmi writes a letter to her sister in Hyderabad. She remembers that it is October and that the *sitaphul* trees in their childhood village are heavy with their burden of ripe, green fruit. *Do you remember the village at this time of year?* she writes in Telugu. *How I miss that delicious fruit—there is nothing here to match its sweet white sugary taste. When I describe the bumpy green skin to the people at the food market, they smile—almost laugh at me. Well, perhaps it is my accent.*

The phone rings suddenly. Lakshmi almost jumps in her chair. "Hello?" she says.

"Mom, it's me." Sridher's voice.

Lakshmi is not happy. Three days ago, she phoned her son at home in the evening, but he was already asleep. Her daughter-in-law explained that he had been on call. But Lakshmi did not sense any respect or love in her voice, only irritation. She had told her son about this feeling before. But he, too, was starting to use that same tone of irritation sometimes. It made her feel like not talking to him at all. "Do you have the day off today?" she asks.

"No, no. I am calling from the hospital. To say hi."

"I was just going out," Lakshmi says, not knowing why she is lying to her son. "I will call you in the evening," she says curtly.

Sridher mumbles a puzzled good-bye, and she hangs up. She sits for a moment in the chair beside the phone, looking through the window at the crimson-leafed maple in the front yard. It stands in startling contrast to the clear blue sky. A breeze filters through its branches and some leaves flutter gracefully to the ground. Finally, she slaps her thighs and stands up. "It is a beautiful day," she says out loud to herself. "I might as well not make myself a liar."

It is chilly today, and for the first time in fifteen years, Lakshmi thinks it is too cold to go walking to the library in a sari. Even as she looks inside her closet, her boldness surprises her. But her children are grown—she no longer needs to impress upon them the Indian culture. There is one pair of black pants that she bought two years ago, just in case she might need them one day. They were on sale for twelve dollars at a discount clothing store. She rummages through Venkat's closet and finds a sweater that is small for him.

She looks at herself in the mirror. The pants fit loosely and make her bottom look too large; the thick sweater hangs midway down her thighs. Perhaps she is not as fashionable as Edna Regan, who lives across the street, but she has lived long enough in this country to wear these clothes. She puts on her coat and locks the door behind her.

Mr. Filian is not at the library. For a moment, standing in the lobby in front of the circulation desk, she is undecided about what to do.

"Laksheemi!" Lucia Stern calls from behind the desk, mispronouncing her name in the familiar way. "Don't we look casual and comfortable today!"

"Oh . . . yes," says Lakshmi vaguely, feeling self-conscious. She steps up to the desk. "Is Mr. Filian still ill?"

"So he says. But I thought you would know if anyone would, Laksheemi. But of course, he's not so much physically ill as down in the dumps. Did you know his mother was very sick and in the hospital? You would think that he would go visit her instead of sitting here doing nothing."

"Mr. Filian is very dedicated to his mother in his own way. I have seen that, Lucia."

"No doubt you have. All I'm saying is that she would probably appreciate his company right now."

"Lucia, would you be having his telephone number?"

Lucia hesitates. Her gray eyebrows stretch into arches above her dull eyes. "Really, Laksheemi, I'm not supposed to give such information. I'm surprised that you don't have his number already—"

Lakshmi is alarmed by the insinuation. She begins to protest, "What do you—" but is suddenly quiet, because Lucia is holding out a piece of paper with the number. She is already helping the next person in line.

Lakshmi takes the paper out of Lucia's hand. As she leaves the library, Lakshmi realizes that she is angry. Angry with Lucia for noticing her clothes. Angry with herself for having to ask for Mr. Filian's phone number. Angry with Venkat for . . . what?

When Lakshmi phones Mr. Filian the next day, she tells herself it is out of genuine concern for his well-being, and for no other reason. Her hands shake as she dials, and this surprises her. The phone rings four times, five, six, before Mr. Filian answers.

"Hello, Filian here."

"Mr. Filian, this is Lak— Mrs. Chundi. It's quite unusual for me to phone. But how are you doing, Mr. Filian? Is everything all right?"

"Mrs. Chundi. How nice of you to call."

Lakshmi suddenly feels giddy. Her mouth starts moving as though of its own accord. "Everyone has been so worried about you, Mr. Filian, everybody. We all are wondering what must have happened to you. The last time we talked you were so anxious . . ."

"Ah, you are a true friend."

"Have you seen a doctor? Are you ill?"

He hesitates. "I cannot lie to you. I have not been ill, a cold and slight fever, yes, but not more than that."

She imagines Mr. Filian's thin face on the other end of the line, the telephone only inches away from his mouth. She thinks how close the telephone is to her own lips. Then she remembers his expression two days ago in the library. "How is your mother? Have you gone to her?"

"She is not doing well, Mrs. Chundi. I fear that going to see her with this cold might do her irreparable harm." There is silence for a moment, as if both Mr. Filian and Lakshmi are assessing the plausibility of this explanation. "Why must I go see her? What good would it do? What purpose would it serve?" His voice sounds exasperated, as if he has been trying to answer these questions himself.

"Mr. Filian, if I may say so, this is not good. Not good at all." Lakshmi feels as if she is lecturing to her sons. But unlike Sridher and Sharath, Mr. Filian does not ignore her, or say meaningless words to console her.

"You must get better so that you can visit your mother," she continues. "With your visit I think she will feel so much better that she may even come back to Boston with you. She can see the library for the first time."

"I can only imagine the disastrous condition of the library."

"Lucia does seem to be lording it over the place now," Lakshmi agrees.

"Ah, she presents as good an incentive to recover as any. That woman has been waiting for this opportunity for a decade!"

Lakshmi finds herself giggling. She cannot remember the last time she laughed like this. Was it with her sister on her last visit to Hyderabad?

"Mr. Filian, tomorrow I have some spare time. May I come with some chicken soup?"

"Oh no! I could not presume to impose upon you like that."

"It is no trouble at all. I will come at twelve-thirty. I made the soup today and there is so much that it will just be wasted."

After she hangs up the phone, Lakshmi walks into the

kitchen, looks around, and considers that she has never made chicken soup in her life.

"What are you going to do today?" Venkat asks the next morning, while eating toast at the breakfast table.

"I will mail some samosas to Sharath. Who knows what he is eating of that college food?"

"Sridher called me yesterday at the office. He said that you were in such a hurry to go out you couldn't speak to him."

Lakshmi feels a clamp tighten around her throat. Why did everyone suspect her? "I was in a rush because it was getting late and there was nothing for dinner. I was writing a letter to my sister."

"I don't know why you write letters." He opens the newspaper. "Can't we afford a simple phone call?"

"A letter lasts forever." Lakshmi takes a bite of her toast. "Don't you remember the letters you wrote me when we were young? I still have them."

Venkat peeks at her from behind the newspaper. He grins sheepishly.

"Now who is saying that phone calls are better!" she says, smiling.

When he leaves for work that morning, Venkat kisses her on the cheek.

Lakshmi spends the morning making samosas for Sharath, then drives to the post office to mail them. On the way back, she stops at the grocery store to buy a large bowl of ready-made chicken soup. At home, she transfers the soup into a plastic container.

Mr. Filian lives in a middle-class section of Lexington, not far from the library and Lakshmi's house. Lakshmi has been there once, five years ago, when she and Sridher gave Mr. Filian a ride home during a rainstorm. Identical houses, painted slightly different shades, sit among dignified maple and oak trees.

It is October in New England. Red, yellow, and violet leaves splash across the ice-blue sky and decorate the dull concrete below. Once, during a visit to Hyderabad, Lakshmi tried to describe autumn to her sister. She told her about the music of dry leaves tumbling along the pavement and the brightness of coral-colored trees against a perfect sky. Her sister couldn't understand. It was much like trying to explain the monsoon to a New Englander: one can carefully describe the physical properties of the season, one can relate all factual details, but the mood, the essence of it remains unrevealed.

Lakshmi rings the doorbell and Mr. Filian answers almost immediately. He wears a blue turtleneck and khaki pants with a belt. Despite his careful attire, he looks ill; his cheeks are bloated and there is red, chapped skin around his nose.

"Mr. Filian, hello!" she says, overly enthusiastic. She extends her hand, but she is standing so close that she needs only to move it by a few inches, and the movement is awkward.

"Hello, Mrs. Chundi," he says, clasping her hand between both of his. "I've never seen you in Western clothes before. It's very becoming."

Lakshmi Chundi blushes. She is surprised at Mr. Filian, and thinks that he is much more forward when not at the library.

"Let me take your jacket," he says.

"No need, I won't be staying—"

"Of course, how stupid of me. I don't want you to catch my cold. You should go."

"No, no, it's not that."

He looks at her.

"Of course I'll stay. I thought that having company might make you more tired."

He leads her into a sitting room. Three walls are lined from ceiling to floor with bookshelves. To Lakshmi, the slightly musty odor of the old books is pleasant. One worn sofa is positioned against the empty wall. A large hunter-green chair with deep cushions is on the other side, accompanied by an old-fashioned floor lamp. She can imagine Mr. Filian in this chair, devouring book after book at a pace that she envies. Three cats sit on the rug nearby and barely look up when she enters.

"You have *three* cats?"

"Actually, I have eight. Let's see if we can find the others."

"No need—"

"Alexander! Picasso!" Mr. Filian calls as he walks into the kitchen with Lakshmi behind him.

She sees six large bowls placed on the floor in the corner, three of them filled with food, the other three with water.

"Tutankhamen! Joan! Mumtaz!"

Two cats immediately appear, and Mr. Filian bends to scratch them delicately behind their ears. "This is Joan—Joan of Arc. And this is Mumtaz."

"Mumtaz?"

"Too much is made of the emperor who built the Taj Mahal, and not enough of the woman who inspired it, don't you think?"

"They're both so . . . pretty," Lakshmi says, but she does not pet them. She has always considered cats to be bad luck. The only cats she has known were the ones that lived in her childhood village to keep the mice away. At least they were useful.

"Would you like some tea?" asks Mr. Filian.

"Yes, please . . . but look at me, I have brought you food because you are sick and now you are serving me. This is quite ridiculous. It is lunchtime, you must eat something." She opens the bag and brings out the plastic container full of soup.

"How can I heat this up?"

"I'm afraid that we'll have to do it the slow way, on the stove top. I don't own a microwave."

"You sit down and rest, Mr. Filian. I will take care of the tea and the soup."

They sit in two chairs in the backyard, under the shade of a large maple tree. The tree is thick with amber-hued leaves that also blanket the lawn below; the long branches float high above the roof of the house. Underneath, Lakshmi Chundi and Elias Filian bask in a yellow-red haze, as romantic as the glow of candles. The leaves have changed the sunlight, softening its glare to gentle luminosity.

Mrs. Chundi describes her childhood in an Indian village south of the city of Hyderabad in Andhra Pradesh, India. She grew up in a huge house with sixteen cousins. She tells him about running barefoot through the rice fields and following the cows as they wandered around the hillside. As she remembers, her face grows soft and radiant. Mr. Filian thinks she looks almost as young as the first time he met her, fifteen years ago. Her hair, now bound in a loose bun, frames her face gently.

Her *bindi* is smaller than it was then, a small fashionable peck that accents her doelike eyes.

Mealtimes in her childhood home were chaotic; three aunts spent the whole day in the kitchen to feed the combined family. In the summer, when it was too hot to sleep indoors, the children slept side by side on the roof at night. During the afternoon naptime, she would sneak off to a little room at the back of the house and read. Although she had passed only the tenth class, she became very good at reading English. Her husband was always surprised at the difficult English books that she understood.

Lakshmi notices that some of Mr. Filian's color returns and his eyes brighten as she speaks. He smiles at her anecdotes. He envisions the life that she describes. He does not think about his dying mother. She knows that he is watching her laugh, and it makes her laugh more. She cannot remember ever talking about herself this much, not with her husband, or her sister or her mother. Certainly not with her sons.

She comes to the end of her stories. She was raised to believe that it was wrong for a woman to be too free with a strange man, any man who is not a father, brother, or husband. She looks at him and sighs. "Is it not amazing, Mr. Filian, how far in life one travels? Not just geographically, but in every way."

"Yes, it's very true," he answers, looking sad. "And we don't know it when we're young. We don't know that one morning we'll wake and find ourselves in a very different place than we ever thought we'd be."

To Lakshmi, who has never told an American about how she misses her childhood, his words reach past years of loneliness and touch the center of her heart. The tears surge to her eyes.

Mr. Filian sees what is happening and fumbles to find his handkerchief. "Lakshmi, Lakshmi! Don't cry. Please don't cry." She takes it from him and gratefully dabs her eyes, embarrassed.

"It is nothing. It is the fall weather, you see, it makes me melancholy, that is all," she struggles to explain. Despite her confusion she notes that he has said her name for the first time, and that he pronounced it correctly.

"Come," says Mr. Filian, rising with renewed energy. "I must show you something."

Lakshmi follows him back into the kitchen, then through a doorway into a greenhouse filled with miniature trees in small pots. Some of the trees' small, knotted branches cascade over the sides of their pots toward the floor; some fan their branches gracefully over their small containers.

"Bonsai trees!" exclaims Lakshmi. "But it must be too cold here for them."

"Bonsai need the cold to live. They require both the warmth of the summer and the severity of winter—the natural cycle of the seasons." Mr. Filian's eyes are sparkling. He looks intently at her face as he speaks. In his enthusiasm, he takes her hand. Lakshmi does not pull it back. "Let me show you the most magical tree of all."

He leads her to the very back of the greenhouse, where a large bonsai sits on a pedestal by itself. The location allows sunlight to shine upon it from three sides. Its gnarled trunk twists gracefully into a crown of tiny green pine needles. On one side, a sliver of white bark snakes along the dark stem. It is old yet strong, perfected over many, many years. Lakshmi gasps.

"Sargent juniper," Mr. Filian whispers, watching her. "She is less than three feet tall, but more than three hundred and fifty years old. The most precious gift I have ever received." Lakshmi walks slowly around the tree, her face moving into the sunlight, then the shadow, as she walks.

"Who gave it to you?"

"An old professor of mine, long ago, when I was in Japan for graduate studies. I had finished almost all the credits for my PhD. Then he died. I'd known him for only two and a half years, but he was a very dear friend, and he did not feel close to any living members of his own family. He gave me this tree while he was in the hospital. It has been handed down generation to generation for at least two hundred years."

"It—she—is so old . . ."

In her mind's eye, Lakshmi imagines a woman finding this tree growing upon a rock two hundred years ago. Perhaps she had grown children, or perhaps her children had died while very young, and she had a husband who loved her very much, or loved her not at all, and the woman carefully removed the tree from its birthplace and planted it tenderly in a decorated pot. Perhaps the tree had been passed down from parent to child since that first woman had collected it from the hilltop, and it adorned the homes of each generation of that family, until the woman's name was a mystery to those who cared for the tree, even though her blood flowed in their veins.

As part of this family, the tree had witnessed the joys and sorrows of the human heart, the inescapable cycle, over and over, generation after generation. The tree had done what Lakshmi could not: it had withstood the harshness and gentleness of each season—and flourished. In that moment it occurs to

Lakshmi that she has lived her life always seeking convenience, traveling the safe middle road which does not bring sweetness or severity, fearing to invite sorrow into her world and therefore never knowing joy, adjusting herself to every circumstance, challenging nothing and no one, not her traditions, not her husband, not herself. She had been a coward; she had never asked Venkat to be the husband he could become. And Lakshmi thinks that the tree, despite its tiny size and dependence on human care, is a far, far greater creature than she.

She looks up suddenly. "You asked me on the phone yesterday why you should go to see your mother, but I was not able to give you an answer. But I know now. We are like the trees, Mr. Filian." Lakshmi looks into the air between them as if puzzled by her own words. "To enjoy the sweetness of the summer, we must live through the winter cold. Otherwise both are lost to us."

The pained look on his face makes her immediately regret her words. "I'm sorry, I've overstepped my limits—"

"No, no. I do believe that with you there are no limits I would jealously guard."

Lakshmi looks tenderly into his face. She feels a hollowness in her stomach, which spreads down her thighs, but she is determined despite her nervousness. She stands on tiptoe and kisses him, shaking, on the lips.

When she pulls away, she is strangely calm. She pats his hand and smiles. "I must be going, Mr. Filian, my husband is expecting me at home." At the door to the kitchen, she turns. "Thank you for such a pleasant afternoon." She walks through the living room into the front of the house, gathers her coat, and closes the door behind her.

It is dusk, perhaps five o'clock. A faint smell of burning

leaves lingers in the air. The trees glow in the angled rays of the setting sun.

When she reaches the door of her car and bends to put the key in the door, she sees the minivan. It is traveling at a normal speed until it reaches her; then it slows, coming almost to a halt at Mr. Filian's driveway. Lakshmi recognizes Vijaya's face through the windshield. For a moment, she is flustered. What will Vijaya think of her walking out of Mr. Filian's home? Wearing pants, of all things? Then, collecting herself, she raises her hand to wave hello. There is no response. The van gathers speed and races down the street. Only then does Lakshmi remember that she was to have been at Amruta's house that afternoon, helping with the preparations for Diwali.

Lakshmi puts the dinner plates into the dishwasher. Venkat is in the sitting room, watching a news show on television. Lakshmi's mind is racing. By now, Vijaya's husband will know. By tomorrow morning, Amruta will know. Then Rukmini and Shailaja and Sujata. At the Diwali party, Venkat will find out. Lakshmi was walking out of the librarian's home, the talk would be. Wearing pants.

"Lakshmi!" Venkat calls from the sitting room.

Affair. The word flashes through her mind. But she did almost nothing. She feels no guilt. Something about this afternoon made her strong. It was not taking tea in the shade of that majestic maple, or wearing pants, or the kiss that she gave Mr. Filian on the lips. It was the bonsai tree.

She shakes her head in disbelief. Is she mad? Is this how fast women justify their adultery? Through visions of strength and mythical trees?

"Lakshmi!" Venkat appears at the door to the kitchen. She drops the plate she is rinsing. It falls into the sink with a loud clatter. She jumps back in surprise. Her hands are shaking. The plate spins around and around but doesn't break.

"Can't you hear?" he says, pausing for only a moment. "I'm calling you. On the TV there is a documentary on the Quit India movement and you are missing. Come quickly!"

The earnestness in his voice touches Lakshmi. Would this be the last night that she is with her husband? "I don't want to watch TV!" Her harsh tone surprises even herself.

Venkat stops abruptly.

"What do you want to do then?" he asks in Telugu.

"I don't know. Talk something. Anything."

"Talk what?"

"I don't know. What does it matter? The weather. How was your day. See how beautiful the trees are now." She is starting to cry.

"Okay, okay, no cause for crying." His eyes show that he is confused, but he tries to smile. He pulls out a chair at the dining table. "Come, we will talk. I will tell you what I did today."

It is Friday, the day of the Diwali celebration. In the afternoon, long after Venkat leaves for work, Lakshmi walks to the library. Her heart pounds as she enters the building. But Mr. Filian is not behind the circulation desk. Nor is he in the research section or the children's floor. Finally, in frustration, she goes back to the lobby. Lucia is not there today. Instead, Heidi, a young mother who lives on her street, answers her question.

"He came into work very early today, Lakshmi. He checked

to make sure that everything was okay, and then he drove directly to New Hampshire."

"New Hampshire!"

"I'm trying not to make it common knowledge, but he called just an hour ago and told me the news. He will be arranging a leave of absence to take care of some things. His mother died late this morning, Lakshmi, soon after he arrived there. He told me that if I saw you I should tell you 'thank you' from him—you would know what he meant."

Lakshmi dresses in one of her favorite raw-silk saris for the celebration. Diwali is the holiday when good Hindus worship her namesake, Goddess Lakshmi. The goddess is the granter of good fortune and prosperity. How ironic, she thinks darkly, that this night her husband could desert her.

Lakshmi's sari is fuchsia with a purple border decorated with swans, embroidered with a glittering gold-thread design. When he sees her, Venkat wags his head from side to side with approval. "You look smart," he says. He is dressed in the usual uniform for the Indian men at these functions: a button-down shirt with dark pants and a belt.

They arrive slightly late at the Lexington High School auditorium, rush in and sit together near the front, at their usual seats. The Brahmin has already begun the *puja*. His monotone voice chants the Sanskrit *slokas*, he sprinkles the flower petals on the small garlanded statue of the goddess while children run up and down the aisles. Lakshmi sees that the oil *deepam* lamps frame the stage quite artfully. Gopal approaches them to wish them happy Diwali. Lakshmi sees the strained expression on his face. She thinks that he glances at her once too often during the conversation with her husband. When she turns her head to say good-bye to him, she sees Shailaja and Vijaya looking at her from distant seats in the auditorium.

The dance recital begins. Lakshmi recognizes many of the daughters of her friends in the Telugu community. Dressed in rich costumes the colors of parrot feathers, with bells on their ankles and red-tipped fingers and eyes lined in black, they relate favorite Hindu stories: the boy Krishna stealing butter from the kitchen, Shiva's terrible dance of destruction, Rama and Sita in the forest.

Lakshmi is worried about what will happen at dinner. *Do not believe what they say about me.* She feels an urge to touch Venkat on the thigh, but she does not do so. The dance performance ends and the crowd files out to the gymnasium for dinner.

Men eat first, and the women fall back politely as the men gather in a line behind the buffet table. Lakshmi talks with her usual group of companions.

"So Lakshmi, you are not wearing pants today," she hears Vijaya say. Her voice sounds muffled to Lakshmi, as if she hears it through a dense cloud.

"Auntie was wearing pants?" cries Rukmini. "They must have suited you."

"Why wouldn't they?" says Amruta. "Don't you think us oldsters can wear pants?"

Lakshmi watches Venkat talking in the buffet line with Gopal. He is laughing at something Gopal says.

"But ask her where she was," Vijaya says to Rukmini.

"Why?" asks Rukmini.

Lakshmi sees Venkat moving away from the buffet line with

a plate of food. He joins Gopal, Harish, and Prakash in a group in the far corner.

"I was at Mr. Filian's house, Rukmini. You must be knowing him. He is the librarian at the Lexington Public Library. He has a bad cold and I brought some soup."

"And what is that?" Vijaya says. "You were supposed to be helping us. Don't you think that people will talk?"

Lakshmi's eyes lock onto Vijaya's face. "Definitely some people will talk. I know that."

In that moment, from the corner of the room, Venkat looks at her. The cavernous gymnasium, the women dressed in heavy silk and jewels, the jingling glass bangles, the running children, the laughing men—all the sounds and colors swirl into a vague mist that forms a background for Venkat's piercing glance at her. Lakshmi shifts her eyes only slightly to meet his. Venkat knows. Lakshmi wonders if the lifetime they spent together, bound by their familiarity of religion and language, by parenting the same children, by sharing the same house, by adherence to the same tradition—will that be enough?

During the ride home, Venkat is quiet.

"I must say one thing," begins Lakshmi.

"Don't say anything."

Lakshmi quivers in the passenger's seat. "I must say one thing," she says more slowly in Telugu.

Venkat is quiet.

She speaks without looking at him. "We know each other. We know each other more than anyone else knows us. You just remember."

Venkat goes to bed that night without a word. When she wakes up in the middle of the night, his side of the bed is empty.

Only for a moment, she is scared. She gets up silently and walks through the dimly lit hallway. He is standing in the living room, looking out the window at the darkness, his hands behind his back.

She can see the profile of his face. He is looking up to the heavens and he is thinking. Lakshmi knows that he is thinking harder than he was the evening that it was decided that Sharath would go far away to Stanford. Harder than the day of the telephone call announcing his father's death in Hyderabad. She turns and goes back to bed.

When Lakshmi gets up in the morning, Venkat is already at the breakfast table, behind the newspaper. She puts some hot water on the stove to make tea.

"Gopal told me last night that the All-India Association is showing a movie tonight," says Venkat.

Lakshmi is suspicious. She does not expect a conversation about movies this morning.

"It is *Bis Saal Baad*," he continues, peeking out from behind the newspaper. "Do you remember that movie?"

"It is one of my favorite movies," says Lakshmi softly.

"Yes—" Venkat pauses for a second, his eyebrows knit together, as if puzzled because he does not remember this information. "Shall we go then?"

"Why not?" She looks at him. Almost imperceptibly, he smiles.

THE VALIDITY OF LOVE

My friend Supriya and I had been roommates in the South End for two months when the letter came from her father about arranging her marriage. It was in a simple white business envelope, and because we had known each other since we were six years old, I read it at the same time she did, standing at the kitchen counter, looking over her shoulder. *Women have certain urges,* Gopal Uncle had written. *These are natural and part of life.*

We looked at each other and groaned. "I thought *Indian* women didn't have urges," Su said stoically.

We had just finished college and found jobs, and we felt unbound from our parents, who lived only twelve miles away in Lexington. We had a Ganesha that hung on our threshold, and an ample liquor cabinet to welcome a steady stream of friends that came for late-night parties and weekend brunches or dropped by after work. We had so convinced ourselves that we were free and hip and American that, when the letter arrived, we were immediately suspicious.

It is the correct time that you should be married in accordance with our customs and traditions, the letter continued. *Your mother and myself would like to help you to arrange a good match.* Atticus, my one-hundred-and-fifty-pound rottweiler, nuzzled Su's leg.

"Help *you* arrange the marriage?" I said. "There's a new approach. My parents should try that one."

We read more. *Enclosed you will find a photograph and CV of a suitable boy. Already I met him while in Los Angeles during my conference, as he is enrolled in his final year as a graduate student at California Technology Institute, finishing his dissertation. He is a brilliant fellow, and I would be proud to have him as my son-in-law. He will be in the Boston area in September for a family wedding. It is best that you should meet him then.*

The photo was of Sameer Murthy, a young man of medium complexion, straight nose, nondescript jaw, average eyes, and a mouth.

"*He* would be very proud to have this guy as *his* son-in-law?" Su said.

"Toss it," I said, with more bravado than I had myself mustered in Su's place, only two months before. "I'm taking the garbage out tonight."

But Su's smooth forehead was furrowed, and she flipped her long black hair over her shoulder. "What makes them change from taking us anywhere we want, buying us anything we want, telling us we're capable of doing anything in the world—to *this?*" she said, shaking the letter as if she were angry with me.

"Marriage is most important for young girl," I said in my imitation of a heavy Indian accent, hoping to make her smile.

But Su was serious. "Why can't they see? I've told them already. There're so many things I want to do before I get married." She sat down with a thud on our kitchen stool. Atticus whined and nuzzled her again.

In college, we had laughed this stuff off and gone to the campus pub for a beer. But now it was getting worse. Our parents were getting more insistent.

I tried again with the accent. "One must marry at correct time. Then eggs are healthy. Children are smart."

"Scary thing is, they believe that shit."

"Too much freedom is not good," I added.

She rolled her eyes.

"Duty is beauty, and rights make fights."

I got a small smile.

"Sex act is sacred for Hindus. For vulgar Amrikans, if skin touches skin, it means nothing."

"Would you stop?" she said, but she was grinning finally, and flung the letter on the table between the doors to our two bedrooms, where Sameer Murthy's average eyes watched us as we walked by that evening, wearing our Victoria's Secret bras and low-rise panties. I was surprised to find it still lying there the next day.

The following weekend, Su and I attended the biannual *bharatha natyam* dance recital held in the Winchester High School auditorium. Su's mother, Amruta Auntie, had been my *bharatha natyam* instructor for fifteen years while I was growing up. She always wanted us to attend the dance concerts, because, she said, it was good for her current students to see us there. All of my childhood memories with Su were against the backdrop of these dance lessons, or in the Indian language and culture classes at *Shishu Bharathi* on Sundays, or in our old bedrooms in Lexington, decorated with pink girly things. I tried to come to the dance recitals whenever I could, even when I was in college.

Su and I sat in the third row from the front, so that we could appreciate the facial expressions of the dancers. I always found these recitals entertaining because I had performed all the same pieces at some time or other, and the girls, whether they were sweet-faced six-year-olds or the older teenagers, always reminded me of myself.

Amruta Auntie tried to make the visual impact as authentically Indian as she could: glimmering silk costumes of saffron, scarlet, and peacock blue, white and orange flowers pinned on ebony braids, stage lights gleaming off thick gold belts. For the past five years, she always had the same middle-aged lady singing in her hypnotic back-of-the-throat voice, the same man stamping out the beat of the dance steps on the wooden block. A new soloist, Uma Reddy, performed Lord Nataraja's Dance of Destruction as if she felt the continents disintegrate under her feet and the cosmos open up before her—she was that good. At the end, the girls came out in two rows, with their bells still jingling on their ankles, all smiles and red lipstick and black-lined eyes, and each one joined her palms together in a final *namaste*.

Su and I raced backstage, but Amruta Auntie was already talking to two mothers by the entrance, and she only raised her eyebrows slightly to say hi. A moment later, Vijaya Auntie, whom I never liked, had grabbed Su, and they were talking in hushed voices near the back door. Vijaya Auntie gazed seriously at her, through glasses perched on her very pointed nose. Two little girls chased each other with ankle bells jingling, while one of their mothers yelled, "Kavita, come back and give the necklace!" Four teenagers, giggling quietly in the corner, discussed a young man's unexpected presence in the audience. I smiled at all of it and settled in the dressing room with some mothers to help the younger girls take off their costumes and anklets. I had just undone a little gypsy dancer's braids when Amruta Auntie whispered in my ear.

"Come with me for a second." She held me by the arm and directed me inside the bathroom. Amruta Auntie had always liked me, despite my "rebellion" during high school, which amounted only to purple hair, black fingernail polish, and smoking weed once in the parking lot behind the gym, but even that was talked about in our community. I think she was fond of me because I was a talented dancer and devoted student, even more devoted than Su. Though the dances were based on Indian mythology that was many centuries old, I always found something in my American life that related to them, at least emotionally. Of course that bothered Su sometimes. I'd be even more of a rebel because I felt this connection to classical dance, whereas Su was mostly a model daughter and all the uncles and aunties thought she did everything a good Indian girl was supposed to. But that's how I knew that some core part of me was Indian—because I loved the dance. Amruta Auntie realized this connection; that's why when I was little and I was mad at my own mother, I used to pretend that Amruta Auntie was my mother instead. Now she looked at me in the sick-yellow hue of the bathroom light and I could tell she was worried. "You must be knowing," she whispered.

"Knowing what?" I whispered back.

"Supriya is going to meet that boy this weekend."

"Oh yes," I said, even though Supriya had told me nothing about it since she got the letter.

"In Wellesley," she volunteered, "where this boy's relative is getting married. And you must be knowing when the meeting is?"

"Saturday," I said with confidence.

"Sunday. Do you think that you can give her a ride?"

I groaned a bit inside. How could I politely convey that I was philosophically, morally, ethically opposed to the whole thing?

"She won't ask you herself, Lata, probably she is a bit nervous. After all, her life could be changed completely by this meeting. If we are lucky, it will." Auntie looked thoughtful. "It will," she said again, and I didn't know if it was a hope or a prophecy. There was a knock on the bathroom door. "Just a minute!" she called out. "I don't want us to take her. She'll feel we are too too involved. Of course, Uncle doesn't agree. He thinks if we take her we can give moral support. But I say better we leave it up to her as much as possible."

I thought about how my own parents had recently tried to set me up. I had attended what my father called a "mandatory dinner" at the house of one of my parents' distant acquaintances, where the meeting was arranged. Everybody was there: my parents, my brother—because my parents thought he could help me decide—"the boy," his uncle, and the host, who was a distant relative of the uncle, too. The guy was a Canadian soon-to-be medical school graduate, who was much sought after because he'd placed in an excellent residency program for ophthalmology, which, as everyone knew, was a very lucrative specialty. His family was supposedly from an old line of land-holding *zamindars* in rural Andhra Pradesh. My mother had assured me I had "veto power," but when I exercised it, my father refused to speak to me afterwards. To make things worse, I was still secretly dating Luke O'Malley, who broke up with me only a week after I met the Canadian doctor. But here was Amruta Auntie, at least trying to respect her daughter's sensi-bilities, trying to give her some space. I found myself nodding yes, I would give Su a ride to the meeting.

"Good!" Amruta Auntie clasped her hands together. "Good good good." She hugged me. Then she looked me full in the face.

"Now, tell me, why have you cut your hair so short, Lata? Not more than one inch long all around. Such a pretty girl, why do you do such things? All of your beautiful tresses just gone!"

I couldn't tell her that I cut it right after the failed meeting with the Canadian doctor. That I never wanted to have that long, Indian sex-kitten hair again, and the hair was mine, after all, to do what I wanted with. "It's the rage, Auntie, haven't you seen it in all the magazines?"

She sucked her teeth in distress. "What you girls think of fashion I don't know." I tried to act like it didn't bother me, but a little corner of my heart felt her disappointment.

We left the bathroom and walked into the tumult of back stage. For a moment, I saw the whole room full of girls and young women, their shining black hair and their round hips and the lovely eyes that took in everything. They thought that every opportunity was waiting for them, careers, travel, love, the world; their parents had told them that's why they'd moved to the United States—so they could have these things. But in the end, the talons of tradition would close in. Perhaps they, too, would simultaneously have a failed love affair and a screwed-up marriage proposal that would alienate them from their parents. I felt sorry for them. No, I can't lie, I felt sorry for me.

On the way home in the car, Su told me what Vijaya Auntie had said to her. "She had heard wonderful things about Caltech Guy, and I should be grateful for having this meeting, Lata, that's what she said. As if it's any of her business."

"How does she know about it?"

"Mom told her! No sense of someone's space. Tell the whole world everything about your daughter's private life. It's everybody's business whom I marry." She snorted. "Same thing you went through."

"So you're going?"

"Do I have a choice?"

I let this question hang in midair. It was what we were all trying to answer, wasn't it?

"Lata, would you drive me out there on Sunday?"

"Out where?"

"To meet Caltech Guy. At two o'clock."

"You can borrow my car if you want," I said, then immediately felt bad for saying it. It's true she was taking the easy way out, but I had been in her situation and I had done the very same thing.

"I'm scared I'm going to get there and the weirdness of it will take over. That I'll find myself doing something I don't want to do." She leaned her head back on the seat and closed her eyes. "Our parents used to be so *modern*. You'd help me stay connected to my real life, Lat. You'd help me hold myself together."

How could I say no to a request like that?

*   *   *

My experience with my own family had been terrible. The weekend after the mandatory dinner with the Canadian doctor, my parents had me come home for my favorite brunch of *masala dosa* with *sambar*. I was reluctant to go, because I thought that the meeting would be the sole topic of discussion. But of course I went, and took Atticus with me. The meal was delicious and my parents and brother were in a good mood, and I almost convinced myself that they had forgotten about the whole thing because they didn't mention it all morning.

But when we'd stuffed ourselves full of potato curry and *dosas* and pushed the empty plates away from us, my father said, "Lata, you will be quite pleased to know that we have heard from that boy's family." I felt my face blanch, and my brother, smart as he was, slipped away to his bedroom. It seems the Canadian doctor, Santosh, had said yes.

"Yes to what?" I asked.

"He must have thought you were very pretty and talked nicely, *beti*," my mother said. "And his grandfather was acquainted with your grandfather back home. He's aware that you did very well in college." She brushed a tendril of hair from my cheek. "So he said yes."

I felt a chill in my gut, because I was thinking, too, that he must have considered that I was from the correct subcaste, and that my skin was fair enough so that he could have what he thought were attractive children, and that my father was a doctor, so it would be an appropriate marriage. He probably thought that I'd quit my job as a grassroots organizer, since it was not a "real profession," and make him a comfortable home.

"What do *you* say?" my mother asked.

"I say no." I hated Santosh now, whereas before I had just been indifferent; he had not tried to talk to me alone even once during the whole dinner.

"What do you mean, no?" my father snapped.

"I'm not interested. I mean no," I blurted out, but I didn't really recognize what, exactly, I was saying no to. In my mind I was weighing Santosh against Luke, with his easy way with people and belief that a young woman amounted to more than her skin and good grades and the economic history of her family. And I was thinking about how unfair it was that I could not introduce Luke to them, that I had spent years hiding, bearing burdens that belonged to people in a distant country on the other side of the globe. I had never, in twenty-two years, had the privilege of introducing my mother to a boy that I liked.

"That's not the way—" my mother began, but my father cut her off.

"Just a minute, just a minute." He held up his finger. "Don't be such a hasty girl, Lata. Do you know what his family is back in India? He has lived in Canada since he was ten, and he is an intelligent fellow, and smart-looking even if he's a little short. But with his earning capacity you can continue on with your dance as long as you want."

That was the final straw. The last time we'd spoken about my plan to help Amruta Auntie teach dance classes, he'd told me, "Forget about that dance, forget about that silly job, and get yourself to a respectable medical school."

I pushed my chair away from the table slowly. "I'll dance in my own time and in my own way, thanks Dad. And you can tell his family I said no." I put Atticus on the leash, and we left after that. I'm embarrassed that I lost my temper enough that I slammed the door.

The next weekend when Luke and I broke up, I called them, just to hear a voice that belonged to someone who loved me. They didn't pick up, so I left a message. My brother phoned two days later, to say hi, but we didn't talk about Santosh. And my parents never called back at all.

The Sunday that Su was to meet Caltech Guy was a sunny but cool August day, the kind that makes you nostalgic because it's so perfect. Su and I climbed into my old Volkswagen Cabriolet and she insisted that I put the top down.

"But what about keeping yourself fair-skinned and marriable?"

"Shut uuuup," she said, fiddling with the roof latch.

I had bought the car thirdhand, and my parents hated it, in part because I wanted it over a new Volvo that they offered to buy for me. But I suspect they also didn't like the bumper stickers that I had plastered all over the back end: two from my office at People for the Ethical Treatment of Animals, others from Amnesty International and Greenpeace, and QUES-TION AUTHORITY BEFORE IT QUESTIONS YOU; also, HORN BROKEN WATCH FOR FINGER, and my favorite, SORRY I MISSED CHURCH, I'VE BEEN PRACTICING WITCHCRAFT AND BECOMING A LESBIAN. Atticus jumped into the back and sat on my CD covers and my PETA flyers, and thrust his gigantic head between us in the front, a bit of drool dripping every now and then.

"Your car's a mess, Lat."

"The front seats are clean." Su was nervous, and had dressed in an A-line skirt and a sleeveless mock turtleneck that she wore for casual Fridays at her job with Fidelity in the Financial District. She carried a white cotton cardigan and for jewelry, she wore only the petite diamond studs that her parents had given her for her eighteenth birthday.

"You look nice," I said. "Appropriately conservative."

I could tell from the way she said "thank you" that she didn't want to talk about the meeting, and I could tell, too, that she appreciated showing up in a car like this one, driven by a pixie friend with a monster dog in the backseat, her long hair flying crazily about her. When we pulled into the parking lot, she looked into the rearview mirror and brushed her hair. She barely glanced at me as she said good-bye, and as I watched her walk into the Starbucks I sent all sorts of strength and good vibes her way, because it would take a lot of both for her to keep her spirits intact.

We had agreed that I'd pick her up in an hour, so I drove up to the lake at Wellesley College, put Atticus on the leash and took a walk. This was the spot where Luke had broken up with me two months and three days ago, right here on this very path, next to this red maple tree, after we had spent the weekend with his family for his sister's graduation. Now, in the shadow of the woods, in the mottled sunlight, I kept pretending to myself that I thought I saw him; that's how melodramatic grief will make you, I guess. A mother and two young kids walked past, and in the same place that Luke and I had dabbed our eyes, the boys giggled. "I'm sorry, Lat," Luke had said. He held my hand as if the breakup were against his will, too, but he was sick of "not being able to move forward," whatever that meant. I told myself the relationship had been doomed anyway;

there was no way that we could be together, not unless I was a sixty-five-year-old widow and my parents were dead and all my family obligations—Indian first husband, children, career—had been paid off.

I missed Luke's family, too, almost as much as I missed him. They had welcomed me with a gracious acceptance that I didn't have with my own parents in my own home.

I brooded over his statement—"not being able to move forward"—and wished I had pressed him on it and wondered what it meant. I never told him about Santosh, but perhaps Luke had sensed him. He felt strongly that I should tell my parents about us, and I couldn't, but was that such a big deal? Then there was that other thing. It started to hurt a little when we made love—although I didn't call it that with him, I called it having sex—but was that such a big deal, too? I went to the doctor and she said there was nothing wrong, nothing at all, so I didn't tell Luke about it. But he knew. And I knew he knew.

"I don't get something, Atticus," I said. He plopped himself down on top of my foot and looked at me, refusing to move from the sunny patch of grass. "No, strike that. I don't get a lot of things." I bent down to pet him, feeling sorry for myself, and he did his usual trick of shoving his massive nose into my thigh. He weighed fifty pounds more than me and could knock me over, but nothing had ever made me regret rescuing him from the pound two years ago, a month after I started seeing Luke.

I went back to pick up Su right on time, and she came out of the Starbucks looking relieved.

"How'd it go?"

"Fine." She shrugged. "He seemed nice enough. We talked about movies, books, food."

"And?"

"And what?"

"And how'd you leave it?"

"We both agreed that the other seemed nice, but that you don't marry every nice person you meet, and that we didn't want to get married this way."

"You agreed on that?" I was impressed that she defined the situation so clearly.

"We agreed on that." She turned on the radio, end of discussion. "Where'd you go with your free hour?"

"Nowhere."

"Lata."

"Really."

"You went to the lake, didn't you?"

"Okay. I don't talk about Sameer Murthy, you don't talk about Luke O'Malley."

"Fine."

"Fine."

We were quiet for the rest of the ride, but by the time we'd pulled up to our street in the South End, I could tell that we'd both enjoyed the wind and the sun and the comfortable silence between us.

One evening when she knew that Su was working late, Amruta Auntie called me at home.

"What is it you young girls want, Lata? Just tell me that."

I could tell from the tone of her voice that it was a good time for me to say nothing.

"Nice education, nice looks, nice family, and still she says no! So what if he grew up in India? What is this American love love

love? In Indian marriages the love starts after marriage and stays forever. In Western marriage the love happens before the marriage and disappears after two years. Then what will you do?"

"It's not like that, Auntie," I managed to say.

"Do you think we're like these American families, leaving you all alone to try to find your own husband? We care too much about you. That is the problem."

"Maybe she feels too young to get married," I ventured.

"We don't leave you to marry any old Tom Dick and Harry who'll cheat on you and not provide for you."

"Yes, Auntie," I said.

"Don't you know that all the rich corporate families in America, all the European royalty get married like this only? Tell me, what is wrong with it?"

But after that there was no talk about Sameer Murthy. Labor Day came and went, the students came back to the city, and Su and I were both wildly busy at work. We went out with our friends to bars in the South End and Back Bay, and even tried a couple of new ones in Central Square. One night we both got so drunk and were out so late that we had to borrow cab fare from a bartender, who knew Su from her office, and Su threw up in the trees in front of our building because she couldn't make it inside the house fast enough. She was like that that week. There was a lot going on inside her head.

The next day was Sunday and Su spent most of it nursing her hangover, sitting with Atticus on the couch. Around seven in the evening the phone rang and I picked it up and it was *him*, Sameer Murthy, just like that. His voice was a little nasal and high-pitched, and he spoke with a modern Indian accent, which, if I weren't Indian myself, I'd probably think was attractive.

When I gave Su the phone, she scrunched her eyes and mouthed his name in surprise, but something told me the call was not totally unexpected, because she immediately got up and went to her room, closing the door behind her.

"Well, two can play at that game, can't they, Atticus?" I went to my room and called him onto the bed with me. There had been something that I had been meaning to do for a long time, anyway. I had been wanting to write a letter to Luke, or call him, or something, and I sat on the bed with a card that I had bought just for this purpose, pen in hand. What to say to him? I toiled with it for ten minutes, then went out to the sitting room again. No Su. I peeked into her room, and there she was, phone to her ear, lying on her bed, looking up way past the ceiling, like we'd do as teenagers.

Two hours later she was still at it, and I had watched our favorite television show by myself, walked Atticus, and gone to bed. She was still talking on the phone. Every now and then, I heard her giggle.

The next morning she explained: she had forgotten her cardigan at the Starbucks the week before, and Sameer took it with him. He got her number through a mutual acquaintance, and he had called only to find out how to return the sweater to her, but they ended up talking for a long, long time.

"It sounds like you had a nice chat," I said, but my voice sounded accusatory, even to me.

"He's got a pretty good sense of humor, a funny glib way of looking at life."

"Who was the mutual acquaintance—your father?"

She gave me a dirty look, a look so mean I don't remember

her looking at me that way since I stole a dance solo from her when we were seventeen.

From that night on, it seemed like I had lost Su to these phone calls. She was holed up almost every night in her bedroom with the phone to her ear for more than an hour. We still talked, and we still went out, but we got along best when there were others around. When it was just the two of us we discussed Atticus, or made a fuss about his drooling, or told stories of what he did that day when the other person wasn't there. I have to admit that my attitude didn't help, either, but nothing prepared me for her announcement two weeks later that she was going to visit a childhood friend of ours, Maya Rao, for a week, out in Los Angeles.

"Are you going to see Caltech Guy when you're there?"

She had her clothes on the bed and was fumbling with her suitcase.

"Sameer. He's got to get my sweater back to me, doesn't he?" she said lightly, as if I'd believe that was all it was.

I had a miserable time that week. While she was gone, Atticus developed a bladder infection and started peeing all the time. I'd come home every day to a puddle on the floor, because the dog walker couldn't always time her visits perfectly. Then I'd spend the evening watching TV and flopping around on the couch, sometimes not answering the phone when it rang. I told myself it was because I wanted to enjoy the time I had there alone while Su was away, but I knew it wasn't that. Perhaps I was jealous of her, but it wasn't just that, either. I was bothered by Su running out to California on the one hand, and by Luke on the other. I still hadn't sent the card, still hadn't figured out what it was I was trying to say.

On the third day I went out to Amruta Auntie's dance studio after work and started teaching a young beginner's class as we had agreed. It helped being with the six-year-olds, beating out the familiar rhythms with my feet, watching as they tried to imitate me. I stayed for a half hour longer than I needed to, fussing with the dance tapes and even sweeping the floor. Finally Amruta Auntie told me, very nicely, that I should leave and get back to the city.

At night I'd lie in the dark and imagine Luke there, cuddled up next to me, or kissing my breasts, or whispering in my ear. And I remembered how it had started to hurt when we made love, what I had been thinking of then, and I decided I hadn't *thought* anything—it was more of a gut sensation, a sudden catching of my core organs, deep inside. There Luke and I would be, naked, seeking some union, legitimate or not, and suddenly the faces of my family would materialize out of the shadowy corners of the ceiling. I saw us as they would've seen us, with his white hands on my dark body, and I realized that it was hopeless. What I'd been trying to give my lover was not mine to give anyway; it belonged to them, to those faces on the ceiling. Luke would whisper, "What's the matter?" and I wouldn't really have an answer for him, just some words jumbled together that, if you were really listening, wouldn't make any sense. Near the end, he wouldn't even ask me at all, he'd just hold me for a while, or worse, turn away. It was all tied together for me somehow—Su running out to California as if she had no life in Boston, and my parents' faces on the ceiling with Luke naked in my bed.

When Su came back I picked her up from the airport and I could tell that something was different. I asked her how the trip was, and how was Maya, and was she seeing anyone, and how did she like her job working for Paramount Pictures? Maya was a bit of a hero for us, because she had had the guts to leave the East Coast altogether. I purposely didn't ask about Sameer because I wasn't sure I wanted to hear her answer. Su gave me all the news but she seemed tired, which didn't really make sense, because although it was eleven-thirty p.m. for us, it was only eight-thirty p.m. out in California. She went to work early on Monday, then she was at her parents' house for dinner on Monday night, and didn't get back to the apartment until after work on Tuesday evening. I was already home, cleaning up a last bit of Atticus's pee that I had found dried on the stairwell landing. He had finally overcome the infection and was back to his usual good-natured self.

Su had brought Chinese food from one of my favorite places in the neighborhood and she set the table for dinner and I could tell something was up.

"Lata," she said, looking at me dreamily, "I'm in love."

I always get a little turned off by talk about love in this straightforward way, even though I believe in it and everything. Maybe because my parents have always acted like it doesn't really exist, at least in the way that people state "I'm in love," as if it were something you could touch. So I just looked at her, and hoped my expression wasn't too negative.

"I'm in love with Sameer, and we've decided to get married."

"They forgot the fortune cookies," I said, rummaging around in the bag.

"I'm in love with—"

"I heard you."

She was quiet for a moment, and I knew I was ruining everything, I wasn't able to pull off the happy-girlfriend part of it at all. "Okay, ahhh . . . Okay. Tell me what happened. Everything."

"Aren't you going to be happy for me?"

"I *am* happy for you."

"Doesn't look it."

"I'm shocked, that's all. I mean, you only just met this guy. Just last month you wanted me to drive you to meet him so that you wouldn't feel pressured into doing something you didn't want to do."

"I did not *just* meet him! I've been talking to him on the phone for weeks and really fell for him when I saw him out there. I mean, don't tell any of our folks, but we were basically living together the whole time I was in Los Angeles."

"You were not."

"Okay, maybe we weren't. But we did—"

"Su—"

"Lata, you know I'm not the type to have an arranged marriage."

"But this *is* an arranged marriage! Just because you've been pressured and brainwashed into thinking you're 'in love' does not mean it's not an arranged marriage!" She was looking at me as if what I was saying were preposterous, but I didn't care. I was tired of her rewriting everything, rewriting life so that it always came easy for her, so that she never had to struggle for the truth in anything. "Life is not a stupid Bollywood movie," I said.

She started as if I had hit her. "You're just jealous of me—"

"Like hell."

"You don't even know what love is, Lata, okay? If you did, you'd still be with Luke."

"Shut up." I got up from the table.

"He really loved you, and you didn't take him seriously, and now that he's gone you're moping around as if he were the one that did you wrong. If you believe in love matches so much, why can't you keep one?"

Now that hurt. It hurt so much that I didn't even say anything back to her, I just got Atticus's leash from the closet and went out with him into the warm night air and walked down the Southwest Corridor Parkway, then over to the Public Gardens. I saw a gay couple strolling in the twilight—a beautiful young man holding hands with a rugged-faced, red-haired one—and out of nowhere I was struck with admiration for them, for their belief in the validity of themselves. Just that belief was enough to hold them together. I gazed down the path they were walking long after they had disappeared.

When I returned to the apartment, Su was gone, and so was the suitcase that she usually kept under her bed. I checked the phone messages and the only one was from my mother, informing me—as if I didn't live with Su—that Su's marriage had been settled, that she was complying with her parents' will and wish, and that there would be an engagement ceremony a week from Saturday.

Imagine that. My mother hadn't spoken with me in almost three months, and that was what she called to say.

Su didn't come back to the apartment. On the second night I was still furious with her, and on the third night, a little less so. By the fourth night, I realized that she thought I was judging her; she was right, and I knew she wouldn't come back unless I called to clear that up. I didn't, so there I was by myself, with only Atticus for company, right up until the night before her engagement ceremony. I still hadn't decided if I would go.

I didn't understand why the engagement had to be so soon, then I told myself that the bond between couples in these arranged marriages was so tenuous that matters had to be formalized as soon as possible; you have to hold things together from the outside if you aren't sure that the inside would hold.

There were many things that bothered me about the ceremony, but the worst was that my parents would be there and I didn't know how they would act. There was no pretending that I approved of Su's decision to get married, but I remembered all our childhood wedding fantasies, and I wanted to be with her during the formal engagement. But I replayed the comment she made about Luke and my not knowing what love is and I got angry again; then I felt guilty that she knew I couldn't be happy for her, so I wanted to apologize.

In the end, I decided that I would do the thing for which I couldn't be blamed by anyone for anything, which was to attend the engagement ceremony and make the best of it. So it was already Saturday morning by the time I decided that I'd go, and I quickly dressed in my fanciest *chalwar kameez* and drove out to Lexington to Su's parents' house. I would be only forty-five minutes late, which is nothing for an Indian function.

When I arrived, the circular driveway was full, and a line of cars stretched out on the street in both directions. A garland of banana leaves hung over the threshold and delicate *rangoli* patterns fashioned out of red powder decorated the front steps. A huge portion of the Telugu community had come out to celebrate with Su's parents and Su; she really was going to get married. I realized that very few of my childhood friends would attend, because most had moved out of town and the younger ones, like my brother, had gone back to college. I wished, irrationally, that I had brought Atticus.

As soon as I walked in I snuck into the bathroom and checked the mirror and immediately regretted coming. My short hair looked ridiculous against the regal violet sweep of my Indian clothes, as if it had been chopped off as punishment or out of spite. What had made me think that I could be here, poised and pleasant, while all these parents fawned over Su? But I couldn't leave, either; I wouldn't be able to face myself afterwards.

So, I walked outside to the glorious late-summer day, to the back lawn and the women in their brilliant jewel-colored saris and men in their gray slacks and button-down shirts. Children were running everywhere; boys and girls in silk outfits chased each other while tripping over their *chappals*. The sound of sitar music floated above our heads, above the brick patio and the trimmed grass and the buffet tables set with huge platters of rice and dal and lamb laced with cilantro.

Sameer and Su sat on two low decorative stools arranged in front of a semicircle of white chairs for the guests. A Brahmin sat next to them, chanting scripture, with Amruta Auntie and her friends in attendance handing him fruit and spices or fussing over Su's clothes. She wore a lavender sari that showed off her fair skin, and her curvaceous figure looked lovely and dignified in the heavy silk. The way she and Sameer beamed at each other, you'd believe it *was* a love marriage. Maybe it was—I wasn't sure.

They exchanged rings, then the Brahmin chanted more Sanskrit, then Su sat patiently while the older women filled the loose end of her sari with fruit and rice, all so she would have lots of healthy children. It was supposed to be beautiful and sacrosanct and good, but nothing's good if you're not ready for it—a new baby, a devoted husband, a dream job, or the tree that turns amber too early, while the enchantment of summer is still in the air. I saw my father in a crowd of men, and Gopal Uncle, whom he was speaking with, pointed at me. My father waved and I waved back; I could help him keep his respectability in front of the community, retain the illusion of a happy family, if that's what he wanted. That was the easy part. But inside I hurt too much to do more than that, to approach him with a generous heart.

Somewhere in the mix of people, in the mandatory conversations with parents of my friends, in the mingling required in the buffet line, I came abruptly upon my mother and her friend Lakshmi. Despite herself, my mother smiled and put her arm around me. Something about this light motion, the naturalness of it, made me believe that she missed me.

"So, what do you think of all this, Lata?" Lakshmi Auntie said after giving me a hug. I felt her eyes sweep over my new haircut, but there was no judgment. If anything, she seemed a bit contemplative in the midst of the festivities. "Supriya looks beautiful, doesn't she?" she said. Su and her fiancé had now seated themselves to view a *bharatha natyam* solo prepared just for them. "Perhaps soon we will see you up there also. But don't rush, Lata. There is no hurry."

I felt my mother stiffen, and the natural moment was gone. "It's so nice, isn't it, that Supriya is getting married in the Indian way," my mother said.

"So nice," Lakshmi Auntie agreed.

"Wonderful," I said, then excused myself by claiming that I wanted a good view of the dance performance.

I wandered to the shade of a tree to the side of the makeshift stage, and there was Su's father, hands clasped behind his back, beaming at the large audience gathered on his lawn.

"Congratulations, Uncle," I said. "You must be very happy. You introduced them to each other at just the right time."

"I had nothing to do with it, Lata, nothing," he said, continuing to gaze at the crowd. "What to do if these young people have found each other and are so enthusiastic about getting married? I told Supriya—take your time, no rush. But it is her wish, and we parents shouldn't stand in their way once they have decided upon each other."

He glanced at me for a second, perhaps to see if I believed him. Then he seemed distracted by a group of men standing a few feet away, calling out to them even though their backs were to us. He leaned in close and whispered, "Next time should be you, Lata, you will also be just as lucky. Come, enjoy the dance program," and he was off to join the group. I overheard him talking a moment later. In response to the congratulations, he said something about Supriya being a sensible girl who always listened to her parents, about her intelligence in accepting this match.

The *bharatha natyam* music began to play, and the dancer came out, wearing red silk and flowers in her braid. I recognized her as Uma Reddy, who had performed the beautiful solo of Lord Nataraja's dance of destruction at the recital. Now she became Radha pining for her Lord Krishna, waiting for him in the forest where he had promised to meet her; yet he did not appear. I knew her dance as if it were part of my own body, for

I had performed it myself, and my muscles pulsed in time to the rhythm that she beat out with her dainty feet. In the midst of the hoopla of Su and Sameer and their loving each other, against the noise of culture and tradition and convention, I remembered myself in the woods by the lake in Wellesley. Uma Reddy's dance was about me and Luke. It seemed a singular moment of truth.

Su and Sameer were holding hands as they watched Uma dance. Su was smiling at the performance, then she turned to Sameer and he looked at her and her smile softened. The air around her seemed to shimmer, as if it were made of different stuff than the air surrounding the rest of us. I was suddenly ashamed of myself.

At the end of the performance, Uma presented Su with an enormous bouquet of blood-red roses and I felt my own arms offering these flowers; as she hugged Supriya, I felt my friend's hands on my own back. For it was clear to me then: Su would have the easy Indian husband and the smiles of her elders and the institutions of a six-thousand-year-old civilization, but I would have the dance. Somewhere in our specious, chaotic definition of Indianness, there was room for us both.

I found my way to Su and she said hello as if we had never fought, as if she hadn't abandoned our apartment ten days ago.

"I'm sorry, Su," I said. "I didn't mean to be a jerk."

"It's all okay, Lata. Here, meet Sameer." She turned to him and tugged on his arm like a child. "She's one of my best friends, so you have to like her!" She giggled.

I felt a surge of annoyance that she didn't apologize to me in return, then our eyes met and it didn't matter. I couldn't be mad at her for getting engaged so young; it must have felt glorious to be free of the constraints that we had shared, to not bear that burden anymore.

Sameer shook my hand and smiled. He was older than I thought he'd be, perhaps twenty-nine or thirty. "Any friend of Priya's is a friend of mine," he said warmly, but he said it as if it were the first time he had heard of me, and not as if I had known his fiancée for sixteen years.

After months of not seeing Luke, of dreaming about writing to him, of thinking that I saw him and being wrong, it finally happened in the grocery store. He was picking out a half gallon of whole milk and I was bending over to get some vanilla soy when I glimpsed the sandy blondness of his hair. At first his face looked like a stranger's, then he smiled and it was him again, and we quickly fell into it, the same voices, the usual familiar expressions.

"Go soy, O'Malley," I said, then regretted it. It was a lame opening line, delivered a bit too loudly.

"No way. That fake stuff will kill you."

"It's not fake."

"And they charge you twice as much for nothing. Didn't I have any good influence on you at all?"

We laughed at this, because it was related to a long-standing joke between us and I was glad that he alluded so easily to when we were together. He had been kind to me during the breakup, I realized. He had respected how I felt. He had never lied.

"So what's the news?" he said.

"Atticus had a bladder infection. He was peeing all the time, everywhere. Su wasn't around to help, so that's all I was doing for a while." Did *that* make my life sound lame. "He's better now."

"That's a lot of pee." He shook his head. "Poor little guy. And how's Su?"

"She's engaged."

"Su's engaged!" He took a step backwards. "How old is she? Don't you have to be an adult to get engaged?"

"Twenty-two."

"Who's the guy?"

"Somebody she met through the Indian marriage network. They've known each other for eight weeks. She thinks she fell in love. Her parents think they arranged it. Everybody's happy."

"Then I'm happy for her."

I hadn't expected that. But then I guess that's why I was always so attracted to him. He didn't judge people. He didn't have the baggage that I had, so he could accept some Indian stuff for what it was. Just another way of doing things.

"I like your hair," he said. "It suits you."

"Thanks."

We looked at each other for a moment longer than two people at the grocery store should have looked at each other. I felt the pull of him, the blue eyes and coarse cheeks and tousled hair, like a day of freedom at the beach in summer.

"I'm sorry, Luke."

"For what?"

"For not telling my parents about you." In the end, all our arguments had come down to that one thing. That I was not grown up. That I could not believe in the validity of love.

"I think it would've helped," he said slowly.

I tried to read his answer. I tried to sense if his words had a tiny trace of hope in them, or only regret. "I think it would've been the beginning of everything," I said.

BANGLES

Arundhati's son's home in Lexington, Massachusetts, sat on a tree-lined street near the country club, overlooking a large pond surrounded by willow trees. Clipped box hedges framed the lawn, a three-car garage was tucked tastefully out of view, the windows were cleaned, inside and out, every spring and fall, and in summer, red and pink petunias marked the stone walk leading to the front door. Arundhati stepped into the house with her right foot first, the auspicious way to begin things. It was a habit she had learned in childhood. She was now sixty-nine years old.

Her son guided her through a dim hallway to a carpeted bedroom with matching drapes and bedspread. Everything was clean. Venu smiled and extended his arm, showing the size and luxury of the space. "This is your new room," he said in Telugu.

He might have said, "This is your new city, new country, new life," because he was her only son, her only child, and she was now a widow. She held his arm and smiled at him, to let him know she was pleased. How strong he looked, like a Hindi cinema hero. Already he had overcome the trauma of his trip to Hyderabad one month ago, where he had set the torch to his father's funeral pyre. Venu would be a good son and care for her now. He would not disappoint her.

He put down a suitcase filled with Indian sweets, coconut oil for her hair, homemade mango pickle, and white saris. In the old days, white was the only color a widow would wear. So it would be with her.

Venu's two daughters stood in the doorway to the bedroom. The younger one, Rani, ten years old, pointed her finger at the vase of flowers on the dressing table. "Look, *Nanamma*, I made them for you in school." Arundhati was relieved that her grand-daughter spoke Telugu so easily; she herself understood only a few English words.

She touched the fabric petals of the flowers, then turned to pinch the girl's cheek. "Thank you, *beti*. So sweet. And little Rahul?" she asked. "Where is he?" She was happy to see her granddaughters after four long years, but it was the grandson, the one who would carry on her husband's name, that she most longed for.

"They are on the way," Venu said.

"*Nanamma*, can I make you some tea?" Tara, the older granddaughter, asked.

Arundhati nodded her head, and the girls raced each other to the kitchen. She smiled and settled herself, slowly, because her knees ached, in the armchair near the bed, just as she heard a door open in the front of the house.

"They're here," Venu said, and called to his wife.

Kamlesh appeared in the doorway, her cheeks flushed from the cold, still wearing her overcoat, carrying little Rahul asleep in her arms. "*Namaste, namaste, Athamma.*" She put her palms together even while holding the child. "Sorry we're late, a huge traffic jam and Rahul fell asleep in the car. No, no don't get up." She bent so that Arundhati could see. "I didn't want to wake him because he's been sick recently."

"Yes, don't disturb him," Arundhati agreed. She peered into the boy's face as he slept against his mother's shoulder, his pink lips partly open, his thick lashes perfectly curled against soft cheeks. "Such a blessing to have a boy," Arundhati said to Venu. "He resembles your father. Maybe he, too, will be a chief minister."

"A senator, or a governor," Venu said. He glanced at Kamlesh. It was obvious; Venu loved his wife even more since a son had been born. Arundhati looked away.

Dinner that evening was a Hyderabadi feast: lamb *biryani, raita*, spinach dal, chicken korma, eggplant with peanut gravy, garlic naan, and lemon rice. Afterwards, Arundhati wished everyone good night and walked slowly to her new room, in her new home, in her new city; it was six-thirty in the morning in Hyderabad. She released her hair from its bun, then removed her earrings and necklace and put them on the dresser. The gold bangles remained on her wrists.

She loved her jewelry. It had been placed on her neck and arms and fingers on the day of her bride-making ceremony, fifty-three years ago, by her grandmothers, aunts, and older cousins, women who had journeyed before her through life. She would be a married woman now; she needed to wear the evidence of her status. Her mother had slipped Arundhati's slender hands through the bangles herself: one gold bangle, then five delicate ones of red glass, another gold, another five of glass, another gold, until they were a joyful tinkling mass that covered her forearm, ending in the intricate henna design on her hand. It happened during a small private moment, before Arundhati sat down with the Brahmin performing the ceremony. Her mother had kissed her cheeks and forehead, and hugged her with the passion of a last farewell. The memory made her smile.

On the tenth day following her husband's death, they held the Vedic ceremony led by the Brahmin, before the sacred flame. Then her sister-in-law and her husband's aunt, widows both, led her outside the home in which she had lived with her husband. They sat on the step at the back door, under the pink bougainvillea that cascaded from the roof. The bush had grown and prospered while she and her husband had been in that house, while they had raised Venu there. Inside, she could hear the hushed family conversation, the faint chanting of Sanskrit *slokas*. It was a perfect November day; a soft breeze swept through the *ashoka* trees.

The two widows wiped the vermilion *bindi* from her forehead and replaced it with ash. They slipped the silver toe rings from her feet. They took off the bangles she was wearing, both glass and gold. Arundhati watched as they shattered the glass bangles with the rocks that lay nearby. She broke the last one herself, just as the tears clouded her vision. She slipped the gold bangles back on; she would wear these as assurance of her status as a woman from a family of substance. Then she went inside the house to sit with the relatives. Her son's kindness, the value of the jewelry she owned, and the money that the government paid for her husband's pension—these were the only protection she had against future misfortune.

For three days, while she recovered from the jet lag, they cared for her. Kamlesh brought her tea in the morning. Venu propped up her legs on the sofa. Her granddaughters explained the programs on television. Rahul sat with her quietly at first. She ran her gnarled fingers through his hair and admired the length of his lashes. She was happy she had come to America. Later Rahul ran from the living room to the dining room to the kitchen, and neither his parents nor sisters told him to go outside and play. He jumped on the sofa where Arundhati slept, and woke her. "*Nanamma* wants to sleep, Rahul," Kamlesh said sweetly, but she did not lift her son to the floor. Arundhati believed that it was her exhaustion that made the boy seem irritating, and did not say anything. She believed it was only a weakness of her body.

After four days, she felt much better, and relaxed in an armchair in the family room. Venu and Kamlesh sat side by side on the sofa. "Can you take care of him?" Venu asked. "Can you stay with Rahul during the day?"

She hesitated.

"Remember when Tara was born? You liked looking after her so much," Venu said. "What fun you and Poppa had then. You really enjoyed that visit."

She remembered her only previous visit to the United States, before her son had joined a private medical practice, and the whole family shared his two-bedroom apartment in Brookline. Her husband had just lost the local elections for the first time. She comforted him. She cooked for the family when Kamlesh could not stay awake. She brooded that Tara had not been a boy. "It has been a long time since then," Arundhati said.

"Rahul's catching a cold almost every other week in daycare," Kamlesh said, "and he'll learn Telugu better by staying with you." She glanced at her husband.

Venu leaned forward. Arundhati had always loved her son's eyes. His look reminded her of when she was a young woman, when she bought *kulfi* ice cream for him, or American records, or convinced his father to purchase a scooter. "Come on, Mummy," he said. "What will you do here all day, with no one to take care of?" He chuckled, as if her hesitation were silly. For an instant she was aware of her dependence on him.

Her name was Arundhati. *Fidelity.* The observer of promise and duty. The epitome of wifely devotion. If her husband were alive, what would he think of her doing nothing, looking after no one, not even their own grandson? Venu was duty-bound to care for his widowed mother; could she not make her presence helpful to him?

She nodded. "I will do it," she said in Telugu. "Of course. It is a grandmother's duty."

She closed her eyes and felt weary. Perhaps she had not recovered from the jet lag after all.

On Tuesday of the following week, Rahul stayed home with Arundhati for the first time. Tara and Rani had a holiday from school and were home, too. Kamlesh and Venu left at a quarter to eight, looking clean and fresh, dressed for work. When the door closed behind them, the house seemed too large. Arundhati had forgotten how to play with children.

She sat in the family room and tried her best. "Rahul, let us make something with your Lego set," she said in Telugu.

"I don't know Telugu," he said, laughing.

"You know Telugu. Don't pretend," Rani said. She was playing a game on the computer.

"Go and get your Legos. We will make something," Arundhati said.

But he would not listen. He stood a short distance away, smiling. "Hi, *Nanamma*."

"Don't worry, I'll take care of him," said Tara. She had been standing outside the door and heard everything.

Finally, Rahul sat on Tara's lap while she read to him. Arundhati wondered what she would do when the girls were not home.

Arundhati turned on the television and watched the images flicker on the screen. She did not understand all of the language, but she could decipher the stories. She peeled an orange, and Rahul took some of the pieces.

"What will you have for lunch?" Arundhati asked her grandchildren. Kamlesh had told her that there was dal in the fridge which only needed to be warmed up. Or there were hot dogs, but Kamlesh did not want the children to make a habit of eating junk food regularly.

"I'll make sandwiches," Rani said. Arundhati stood in the kitchen with her hands clasped behind her back, watching the girl.

After lunch, Rahul took a nap. Rani listened to music in her room. Tara talked on the phone. When Arundhati came near, she lowered her voice.

Arundhati went to her own room and lay down on the bed. She began a letter to her brother who still lived in their childhood village home, but fell asleep before she finished. When she woke at three o'clock, she went into the living room and began to watch television. Rani fetched Rahul from his bed.

"Come and sit on my lap," Arundhati said, turning the television off. "I will tell a story."

He stood in front of her, rubbing his eyes. He shook his head. *No.*

"I will tell you the story of the lion and the goat from the *Pancatantra.*"

"I want some juice," Rahul said.

"I'll get it, *Nanamma,*" Rani said. "Don't get up."

Rani opened the fridge. "Uh-oh, Rahul, there's no juice. Tara drank it all."

"I want juice," Rahul said, tugging on his sister's shirt.

"I did *not* drink it all," Tara said.

"Don't worry, little one," Rani said to Rahul, in the way her mother would.

But it was too late. Rahul began to cry. The weeping turned into a wail, his small mouth opened into a circle.

"I'll go to the store, *Nanamma,*" Tara said. She put on her coat.

"How can you go?" Arundhati asked. "You do not drive."

"I'll walk. There's a store on the corner. Otherwise Rahul will just keep crying."

"It will be dark when you get back."

"That's okay. I go all the time."

"No." Arundhati pulled the coat away. "What if something happens? Your father told me to look after you."

"*Nanamma*, I'm thirteen years old."

"Exactly. I forbid you to go."

Tara glared at her. "I can't believe this." She ran upstairs to her bedroom and slammed the door behind her.

Rahul continued to wail. When Kamlesh and Venu came home a few minutes later, he was still screaming.

"She wouldn't let Tara go to the store," Rani said.

"Not 'she,' say '*Nanamma*,'" Kamlesh said.

Venu stood aside with his hands in his pockets, watching Rahul as Kamlesh dried his eyes. Wouldn't he scold his son at all? "Come on, Rahul," he said, "let's get some orange juice."

Arundhati was carried back sixty years. She saw her own father standing there, looking at her brother with the exclusive affection reserved for sons. Oh, her father had loved her, too, but he loved her brother *especially*. She closed her eyes, surprised at the memory.

Kamlesh went upstairs and called to Tara through her bedroom door. Arundhati could make out a few of the words, "—not so bad—tell *Nanamma*." A moment later, Tara walked down the stairs with Kamlesh following her.

"I'm sorry," her granddaughter said, looking at the floor. For a second, Arundhati thought that Tara would touch her grandmother's feet in the traditional way, then realized that she would not.

Suddenly, Arundhati moved forward and hugged her. "*I* am sorry. I do not know anything here." She wondered how, after sixty years, in a living room across the world, she had seen her father and brother again.

*   *   *

One afternoon the following week, Arundhati lay down in her new bedroom for a quick nap, but could not fall asleep. Instead, she sat in bed and continued the letter to her brother, writing the Telugu words with deliberate precision. She wrote to Rajgopal not to worry about her. She felt that she belonged with Venu and the family; it was her karma to be so far away. Everything was as God willed it. *Little Rahul is chubby and healthy and his skin is of a good color—he is our own little mountain of gold!* she wrote, feeling the muscles in her stomach tighten. *Sometimes he is too energetic for me,* she added. *I must become accustomed to small children again.* She asked Rajgopal if he felt safe, returning to live in the old village home. She had heard that some Naxalite thugs had murdered the son of an old *zamindari* landowner in a neighboring district. *We were a kind landlord family in the old days, it's true. But do the villagers respect those distinctions anymore?* She was sealing the letter when she heard a knock at the door. It opened slightly, and Venu looked through the crack.

"I came home early from the hospital. Am I disturbing you?"

"No, son," she said, happy to see him, carefully bringing her feet onto the floor and adjusting her sari. Her necklace slid into place. The gold bangles settled on her arm.

"Did you finish unpacking?" he asked, looking at the suitcase on the floor.

"There are some things left."

He found the remaining saris and blouses, opened a dresser drawer and put them inside. He is a good son, Arundhati thought.

"Did Rahul wake you up just now?" he asked. "He had his friend Dave here—thank god his mother just came to pick him up. He's so noisy, and makes Rahul even noisier."

"*Ramachandra!* How can a grandson disturb his grandmother?" She smoothed her bun. "I was just thinking. I had a wish that your father would see Rahul at least once more before he died."

Her son sat down beside her. "I, too, wished that."

"Why did you not come again, then?"

"There was always something. The girls' school. My medical practice. Kamlesh's clients."

Her response formed in her mind, but she did not say it. *You are an only son*. She did not want to admit that she believed her son was selfish sometimes. They were both quiet for a moment.

"That question has been in my mind for a long time. But we cannot change the past." She put her hand on his. When he looked at her, she smiled. "I was hoping there is a temple near us."

"The Sri Lakshmi Temple in Ashland. It's only thirty minutes away."

"Do you go regularly?" she asked, but she knew that he was not religious, despite her efforts. As a child, he would pretend for her. Now he no longer did even that.

"Sometimes for Diwali."

"Let us go this Saturday—tomorrow," she said. "All of us. Let us go and do a *puja* for your father." He could not refuse. He put his hand on her shoulder. "As you say, *Amma*."

*   *   *

They rode in Venu's Mercedes SUV, with Arundhati sitting in the front passenger seat. When she saw it, she noted that the Sri Lakshmi Temple in Ashland was not like a small Indian temple, made of stone and visited by humans, monkeys, and cattle alike. Nor was it similar to a large Indian temple, grandly situated on a hill, built with marble balconies where the breeze plays with a sari's folds. It was a small American temple. It was made of white stone, built adjacent to a parking lot, and surrounded by the New England woods. A few of the women worshippers, like Kamlesh, wore slacks.

But Arundhati walked inside the temple with confidence; this was her domain. She knew many Sanskrit *slokas* by heart, she could read the Hindu calendar unassisted by a Brahmin. Her son and daughter-in-law followed slowly. Her grandchildren stepped ahead, curious.

"Take off your shoes in the front room," Arundhati said, as Tara tripped over the threshold.

Tara turned to her sister. "Rani, take your shoes off," she ordered, as if irritated that her sister did not know about this basic practice.

"Dad." Rani pointed to Rahul, who was about to run inside the temple's main hall. Venu caught him, forced off his sneakers, and put them on the shoe rack.

"You'll be a good boy today, won't you, Rahul?" Venu said.

Arundhati approached the man standing behind the counter. He was very short, only a little over five feet, and Arundhati could look him in the eye.

"Is there a Telugu Brahmin here?" she asked in Hindi.

"One minute. I'll fetch him."

Arundhati saw her son, waiting, leaning against the far wall.

The girls stood a few feet away, talking to their mother. Tara's arms were crossed, and she shifted her weight from one foot to the other. Kamlesh was stroking the hair away from Rani's face. Kamlesh's back was to the alcove where the statue of Goddess Lakshmi stood. Why was she being so disrespectful?

Rahul ran everywhere. He lingered for a short time with a group of women who sat on the floor, a little distance from the alcove. Then he sprang to his feet and visited two Brahmins talking in the corner. There was a basket filled with coconuts and flowers on the table next to them. When the Brahmins saw Rahul, they smiled. One raised his eyebrows and spoke to him, putting his hand on Rahul's head. But Rahul scampered off. He ran to a man who bent to put money in the collection box, and stared as the man put his palms together in prayer. Then a bell rang and Rahul was at the entrance to the alcove, where a Brahmin held a small flame in a metal dish, holding it out to the people who stood around him. They brushed the flame with their palms, then put their hands to their eyes. Rahul began to mock them—lunging his hand out, then bringing it back in, hitting himself on the forehead, over and over again, laughing.

Arundhati looked away. What nonsense was that? She looked for Kamlesh, but her daughter-in-law was still with Rani, unaware of her son's antics.

The Telugu Brahmin was young, a bit pudgy, and had a thick mane of black hair that was tied into a bun at the back of his head.

"Sir," said Arundhati in Telugu, "I am Mrs. Prabhaker Rao. I would like to do a special *puja* for my husband. He died seven weeks back."

"My regrets," the Brahmin said. His voice was soft, as if he expected her to cry. "You just came from India?"

"Three weeks back. My son is here, I stay with him now."

"That is very good," he said. "But, I am sorry. I can't do another *puja* today. We are too busy on Saturdays, and I do not have all the things I will need." His look was respectful.

"But I have come all this way. My whole family is here. See." She pointed at Venu and Kamlesh, talking near the entrance. "We have come only for this purpose."

"Come back tomorrow. At ten o'clock I am free."

But Arundhati knew her family would not bring her again the next day.

"My husband was at one time the chief minister of Andhra Pradesh," she said to the Brahmin.

"Please, come tomorrow, Mother," the Brahmin said gently.

Arundhati wrapped the loose end of her sari around her shoulders. Her hands shook. In India, she was nothing without her husband. But here, even her husband was nothing.

She made herself stand a bit taller when she spoke with Venu. "He says they cannot do the *puja* today. He told us to come back tomorrow."

"It doesn't matter," Venu said. "We can do it at any time, right? There's no requirement that it must be done today."

"But can't they somehow fit us in now?" Kamlesh asked.

"He says he does not have everything he needs." Arundhati waited, but Venu and Kamlesh did not volunteer to come the next day. She felt a sting behind her eyes. "I will go and pray," she said finally.

When she came back, a young woman was talking to Venu and Kamlesh. Her single long braid hung down the back of her *chalwar kameez*. She was holding the hand of a young boy who seemed the same age as Rahul. Venu introduced her as a friend, Rukmini was her name. She wore a large *bindi* that accentuated the wide space between her eyes.

The woman put her palms together and greeted her in Telugu. Arundhati only nodded.

The conversation continued in English, and Arundhati could not understand it all. Kamlesh laughed at something Venu said and took her husband's hand. Arundhati stepped back from them. Her granddaughters were studying the temple schedule that hung on the wall. Rahul stood near the basket filled with coconuts and flowers. The Brahmins were gone. Suddenly, her son turned to her, speaking in Telugu.

"*Amma*, would you like to come to the temple every week?"

"It would be nice," she said. Was it possible that her son would bring her?

"Rukmini says she comes every Saturday. She'll pick you up. She lives only ten minutes from us." The words paralyzed Arundhati. But Venu was smiling, and Kamlesh, too, seemed pleased. The young woman, this Rukmini, looked at her sweetly. What sort of shame was this? Since when had she needed help from people she did not know?

Arundhati said nothing. Gazing past Venu, she saw Rahul. He had taken a coconut from the basket and was running toward the alcove. He brought the coconut behind his head and flung it, over the seated devotees, into the small chamber where the statue of the goddess stood. Arundhati heard a gasp. Strangers stared with their mouths wide open.

Arundhati ran to her grandson and caught his arm with her right hand. Rahul screamed. She pulled him toward Venu and deposited him, in a heap, at Venu's feet. She could feel her heart beating against her chest.

Kamlesh picked up her son. "Don't you think you're being a little rough?" she said, looking at Arundhati.

"No, it wasn't rough," Venu said. "He's screaming because he knows he acted so badly. Nobody hurt him." His face was serious. "Rahul, be quiet." He put his finger over his lips and opened his eyes wide.

Kamlesh walked quickly to the door, holding Rahul. The girls followed her. Rahul's screams filled the hall, but there were no tears in his eyes.

"I'll call about next Saturday," Venu said to Rukmini. Arundhati walked outside with her son.

In the car, Rahul sat on his mother's lap, in the backseat. Several times, Arundhati turned from the front to look at him, but he would not meet his grandmother's gaze. Kamlesh, too, spent the ride looking out the window. Even Rani and Tara were quiet, and Arundhati felt she had done something very wrong.

"Do you know that girl very well?" Arundhati finally said to her son.

"'That girl'?" Venu asked.

"In the temple."

Venu smiled. "Do you remember Nagpur Reddy Uncle's mother-in-law? Rukmini is her cousin-sister's daughter."

"She is a *kamma* then," Arundhati said, relieved at knowing the family clan affiliation.

"Almost everyone in the Telugu community knows Rukmini and her husband. He is an engineer at Digital. She is active in that group—what's the name, Kamlesh?" he said, looking in the rearview mirror at his wife.

Kamlesh was staring blankly at the other cars on the highway. "*Saheli,*" she said finally, in a low voice, without looking at him.

"*Saheli,*" Venu repeated. "An Indian women's group. They organize outings and activities for Indian women in the area."

"They help women who are being beaten by their husbands," Kamlesh said flatly. She still did not look at anyone.

"That happens here also?" Arundhati asked. "This *Saheli* comes between the husband and the wife?"

"Well, it helps them live together," Venu said. "The point is, she's a very active member of our community. You'll like her."

But Arundhati did not know what to think of Rukmini. After all, why should a young woman, an outsider, involve herself in matters between a married couple? She remained quiet and did not ask any more questions, including the one most important: why her son could not bring her to the temple himself.

The next Saturday morning, Arundhati waited in the foyer, dressed in her white sari, boots, and a long winter jacket. She tucked her bangles inside her sleeve and was annoyed that her earrings caught occasionally on her muffler. She asked Venu for five dollars for the temple collection box. When Venu answered the doorbell, Arundhati did not move.

Rukmini stood on the front step and Venu invited her inside.

"My son's waiting in the car, and we're running late for the ten o'clock *kalyanam*," Rukmini said, and promised to come in on the way back.

Venu helped Arundhati across the ice on the driveway, although she felt she did not need it. When he tucked the end of her sari inside the car and closed the door behind her, she felt she was being handed over, like a burden, to a stranger. Rukmini's son sat quietly in the backseat.

"Comfortable, *Amma*?" Rukmini asked in Telugu. She was wearing sunglasses, like so many Westernized women. Girls in India wore them, too. Arundhati had always thought they were a sign of vanity. "You can move that seat back, if you like."

Arundhati said nothing; she only motioned with her hand that she was fine.

"It must be cold here for you," Rukmini said.

Arundhati stared out the window at the houses. If she answered Rukmini, was she indicating her acceptance of the situation? But Rukmini was being kind. It was Venu and Kamlesh who were to blame.

"Very cold," Arundhati said.

"It takes some time to get accustomed."

She was not a pretty woman, Arundhati decided. Her nose was flat and stubby, her eyes were too far apart, and some hair had escaped from her braid and curled on her forehead and temple. Venu had said that she knew Rukmini's mother's cousin-sister in Hyderabad, but that woman was fair-skinned, tall and lovely. Rukmini was not like her at all.

"You are really Nagpur Reddy's relation?" Arundhati asked.

"Nagpur Reddy?"

Arundhati explained the connection in the way that Venu had. Rukmini confirmed it.

"You do not look like a member of that family," Arundhati said.

Rukmini seemed to be concentrating on the road and said

nothing, but Arundhati thought she saw a shadow of irritation on her face. They traveled for several minutes, while the bare New England trees streamed past them. Arundhati decided that she, too, should act uninterested. Their car turned onto the highway and picked up speed.

But the silence began to annoy her. When she turned to look in the backseat, the boy stared at her with wide, unblinking eyes. "What is your son's name?" she asked finally.

Rukmini smiled for the first time, and Arundhati was relieved. "This is Ram. He's five years old, and a very good boy. Ram, can you say hello to *Nanamma*, sweetie?"

"Hi," said the small voice from the backseat.

"Hi," said Arundhati, fitting her tongue around the word.

"He's shy," Rukmini said. She turned to her. "Sit back, *Amma*. Get comfortable. Think of this as your own car." Arundhati's stomach clenched in gratitude at these words, at the old Telugu manner of welcome.

"I'm very happy that you're coming to the temple with us," Rukmini said. "I hope it becomes a habit. Ram's own grandmother is so far away, it's good that he can meet other elders in our community."

Arundhati looked at her with suspicion. But the young woman was earnest.

"You are a very good driver," Arundhati said.

Rukmini laughed.

"Much better than my daughter-in-law." As soon as she said it, Arundhati was sorry. She should not put down family members to outsiders. Had not Venu said that this Rukmini involved herself too much in the private matters of other families? Quickly she added, "It must be hard to drive so fast while staying within the lines. There are so many women drivers here. They even drive lorries."

"There are not so many differences here between men and women," Rukmini said. "Not like at home. But even there, it's changing."

Arundhati hesitated. "Is it safe to allow a young girl to walk outside when it is getting dark?"

Rukmini glanced at her. "I think so, *Amma*," she said. "At least in Lexington. Things are different here. Girls are not restricted as I was, growing up in Vijaywada."

Arundhati considered this information. She had never worried about Venu's safety when he was young. Of course, boys did not need to be protected as much as girls. As a teenager, he had full freedom to come and go as he wished, even very late into the night. Her husband had never objected.

The car turned from the highway onto a road that Arundhati recognized from the previous Saturday. When they entered the temple, it was as busy as it had been before. But their worship went off without incident, and Ram was very well behaved, and Arundhati admitted to herself that she was glad to have the opportunity to go, even without her son.

As time passed, Arundhati discovered how to care for Rahul. She told him a story from the *Pancatantra* whenever he asked, if she was not tired. She watched him play with his Legos or his train. She put children's DVDs on the television. She made sandwiches for lunch, or, when she was in the mood, she cooked an Indian omelet, with onions and cilantro and cumin seeds. If Rahul stamped his leg to demand something of her, she refused. When there was no more orange juice or milk, she did not make a trip to the convenience store, even though, as Tara said, it was only a ten-minute walk. She would never have deigned to go on such an errand at home, and she would not do it here. Her old legs would not carry her that far, she said; she was too tired. He could do nothing except cry, and she ignored him, because, ultimately, he was more helpless than she.

But when the parents returned at the end of the day, the relationship between grandmother and grandson changed. Rahul became bolder. He pretended not to hear what she said. He hid her slippers. When he walked past her on the couch, he would step on her foot on purpose.

"Rahul, you'll go blind, little one," Venu would say. "You shouldn't step on an elder."

"It is wrong," Arundhati would add. But Rahul did not care. He would run to get a dish of ice cream from his mother, or a kiss, or some sign of sympathy. Arundhati noticed that Venu and Kamlesh spoke with her less frequently, and played with their son more. Sometimes, when she walked into the sitting room, Venu and Kamlesh would stop talking. There were days when Kamlesh would not speak to her at all.

"He is disrespectful to me," Arundhati said once to Venu, as they were watching television. Kamlesh was not in the room.

"He doesn't mean it. He's just a child."

"But you allow him to do it."

"It's no more than what you allowed me." His voice was sharp.

"Your father was very strict." Even as she said it, she realized it was a lie.

Venu was silent. His eyes wandered back to the newscast on television.

"I do not think I can tolerate it anymore, son."

"Are you saying that you won't take care of him?"

The finality of the statement—its impossibility—shocked her. "No—that is not what I mean," she said. But she returned to her room, and lay on the bed, and wondered if it was.

At first, she was certain that, as a child, Venu had acted very differently from Rahul. But then she remembered how she had stopped playing the sitar because Venu craved her attention and would not let her practice. She had given her son everything he might want, before he asked for it. She had dressed him in the finest clothes and her husband had sent him to the best schools; he had even talked to the dean to have Venu admitted to Gandhi Medical College. Venu was the only son. Treasured. She did not have the energy to do it all again.

On Saturday, she asked Rukmini if Americans did not care for their elders. "Everywhere I look, it seems that young people are disrespectful." As an afterthought she added, "Not in my own family, of course."

"That's what we Indians say, *Amma*," Rukmini answered.

"You do not agree?"

"I think Americans care for their elders just as much as Indians do. In India, we make more of a show of it."

Arundhati considered this.

Sometimes, Venu's and Kamlesh's friends invited the whole family to a large dinner party in a private home, where the Indian food was served buffet-style, and the ladies wore silk saris and sat in the old way, separately from the men. Venu felt these were good parties for her. Where else could she meet other women her age who shared her culture?

But she did not enjoy herself. She watched the young ladies with short black hair and golden skin, wearing shimmering fabrics of orange and pink and red. These women talked of their careers, and boasted about their children, and complained about their husbands while smiling good-naturedly. They planned trips to France and Kenya and places she did not know, and even spoke knowledgeably about politics.

But Arundhati sat quietly with the older women and other widows. They talked about jewelry, or the weather, or about the complexion of the bride at a recent wedding. What did Arundhati have to say to these people? They had not been her peers when her husband was chief minister. They had not been the companions whom she knew before her marraige. How silly her son was. Did he think friendship was once more possible for old women, who, long ago, had allowed it to fade away?

She sat alone in her bedroom, writing letters to her brother, remembering. Her childhood home in the village. The draped palanquin in which she traveled. The old sitar that lay, unstrung and warped, under her childhood bed.

Kamlesh was not a good cook in all respects, but she made delicious *dosas*. The batter was always thin and light, and spread like lace on the cooking pan. When she wrapped the *dosa* around potato curry, her Saturday-morning guests were always delighted.

Prakash and Malini arrived with their baby at ten o'clock. He was a cardiologist whom Venu knew from the hospital, and with his broad shoulders and long legs, he reminded Arundhati of a Sikh warrior. They lived in Lexington and were among Venu's and Kamlesh's closest friends. The couple sat in the living room across from Arundhati and smiled while she answered their questions. She was waiting for Rukmini to take her to the temple.

"You're making a relationship with the children," Prakash said to her in Telugu. "Very good. It doesn't usually happen these days."

"Children don't even know their grandparents anymore," agreed Malini, "especially when we're living halfway around the world." She looked at her baby, who had fallen asleep on her shoulder. "Prakash's parents are no more. But I hope this little one will at least know his mother's parents."

Arundhati nodded her head.

"*Amma* is helping *very* much," Venu said. His voice sounded louder than usual. Arundhati knew that he meant to be kind.

Kamlesh rose abruptly. Arundhati saw Venu look at his wife, but Kamlesh avoided his gaze. "Malini," she said, "I'll show you the new bedroom furniture before I start making the *dosas*." Malini followed her upstairs.

Arundhati felt uncomfortable sitting with the men. "I will check the potato curry," she said.

In the kitchen, Rahul sat at the counter, his coloring book and crayons in front of him. A vase of tulips stood nearby. It was made of heavy crystal and caught the sunlight from the window. Rahul had taken out one flower and, holding it by the petals, was waving it about, sprinkling water everywhere.

"No," Arundhati said, "stop that."

Rahul dipped the tulip in the vase and waved it again, pointing it at her.

The doorbell rang. Arundhati heard Rukmini's voice in the foyer. Kamlesh and Malini were coming down the stairs. Again Rahul sprinkled her with the water. Arundhati walked around the counter and put her arm around his waist, to lift him down from the chair. Rahul screamed. His hand caught the vase—deliberately, it seemed—just as Arundhati lowered him to the floor. A loud thud rang out. The vase had tipped off the counter, landed on the kitchen tile and broke neatly into four large pieces; water splashed the cupboards and drenched the floor. Arundhati looked up. For a brief moment, before they understood what happened, Venu and Kamlesh, Prakash and Malini and Rukmini stood in the kitchen, staring at Rahul, at the vase, at the water, at her. She heard her granddaughters running down the stairs.

Rahul looked at all of them, frightened. Then he opened his mouth and screamed, "She did it!" pointing his finger at her.

"Rahul—don't lie," Kamlesh said.

"She did it!" Rahul swung his foot back and kicked his grandmother in the leg.

"Rahul!" Venu's voice boomed.

But it was too late. Seven pairs of eyes had already witnessed Arundhati being kicked by her grandson.

In the car, Rukmini said nothing. Even Ram, sitting in the back, was quiet. Rukmini put her hand on Arundhati's as it lay in her lap, and from this simple gesture, Arundhati began to cry. "Do you know," she said, "when I was a young woman, my father named one of his villages after me. It was part of my wedding present, along with all of the jewels as dowry. That is the life I led then. That is the past I came from."

When she came back from the temple, Arundhati immediately went to her bedroom and lay down. She did not answer the calls for her to come and sit with the family. She did not have dinner with them. Venu knocked on her door after they had eaten, after the children were in bed.

"Come inside and talk with me," she said finally.

Venu sat down on the bed beside her. The lamp on the nightstand shone on one side of his face.

"I have been thinking very seriously," she said.

"Rahul did not mean—"

"I want to go."

Venu swallowed. "Go where?" he asked.

"I want to go back."

"Go back where?"

"To India. To the village. I will stay with your uncle." She imagined that her words, uttered quietly, with no deference to custom or duty, could set her childhood home ablaze.

He stood up and looked at her. "It's not safe. The villagers are rising up against all the old landlord families—they have guns. You heard what happened to Narasimha Rao just last week."

"My brother and I could live happily together. The house is in good condition. There is running water, and a new hospital nearby, and I would have your father's pension. I could play the sitar again, after all these years." She looked at him. "Do you remember, I used to play the sitar?"

Her son shook his head, almost imperceptibly. "You could play here."

She swallowed, and looked away. "I am old. But I can still walk in those fields again, like I did as a girl. I can watch the sun set over the rice plantations and the red boulders. I can pick tomatoes at dawn and eat them for breakfast. We were a kind family in the old days, Venu. The villagers will not harm us." She reached out to hold his hand. "My brother has told me to come," she added quietly.

Venu looked up. She saw he was surprised that she had confided in her brother.

"Ridiculous," he declared, still looking down at her, his hands on his waist. The Hindi cinema hero.

"But I am in the way here. I am not a help to either you or your wife. And she does not want me here, either, I think. You must respect her wishes too. Perhaps the Indian way of family living does not work here."

Venu pursed his lips. She knew he was furious. "A son should care for his parents, *Amma*," he said, as if he had been insulted, as if her suggestion was unnatural. "What more can I do for you?" He spread his arms and indicated the comfort surrounding them. "What are you asking for?"

"I want to go. I am asking to go back."

Venu paused. "*No,*" he said. He closed his eyes, and Arundhati saw him take a deep breath. "Your place is here."

There was silence for a moment, while her situation grew clear. It was impossible, going back; who would bring her suitcases from the basement, drive her to the airport, purchase the ticket? She did not speak the language. Her husband's Indian pension translated into a few dollars a month. For a moment she saw herself as she must look to her American granddaughters: a small lady wearing a white sari, thin hair caught up in a bun, wandering through a shopping mall, or on the sidewalk of their clean neighborhood, or in the McDonald's restaurant. Burdened always with her utter dependence. She realized it with surprise; she cared what Tara and Rani thought of her.

"What would people say, *Amma*, if you went back? What if you were hurt in the village? How could I live?" Venu stood there for a while, but she had no answer for him. When he left the room, Arundhati did not say good night.

Later that evening, when she got up to use the bathroom, she heard Venu talking to Kamlesh in the living room. In the darkness, the words seemed to echo in every corner of the house.

"*Amma* said that she wants to leave. She wants to go back to India, to live in the village with my uncle."

Arundhati did not hear Kamlesh answer. That silence seemed most fantastic of all.

She thought about it during the week. While watching Rahul or eating dinner with the family, she considered it all. At night, she closed her eyes and asked her husband. But her vision of him, in his Nehru jacket and white cap, did not answer her. Must she decide alone, with no one to help her? The thought made her shiver. Yet the decision came like a great bird descended from a far-off place, and it could not be tempted away. She would go against duty and custom. She would tolerate the criticism of her relatives and family. She would take the first step, the first action, for the first time; then, perhaps Venu would be convinced.

On Saturday morning Rukmini arrived as usual. Arundhati climbed into the car and sat looking at her, assessing how the young woman would answer the request. She wondered if she was asking too much.

"You are my friend, aren't you?" Arundhati said. For a moment she envisioned Venu as a boy, gazing back at her with his lovely eyes, and she felt a sharp ache of regret.

Rukmini hesitated. "Your *friend*, *Amma*?"

"I know. There is such a difference in age." A woman of sixty-nine years could inspire respect, or indifference, or perhaps affection. But friendship, that was a privilege of the young. "You are my friend," Arundhati insisted. "You care for my welfare."

"I care for your welfare," Rukmini agreed. "I care if you're happy."

Arundhati felt a familiar sting behind her eyes. "Then take these." She slipped the gold bangles off her wrist. "We need not tell anyone. Take them and sell them for me."

"*Amma*, why?" Rukmini whispered.

Arundhati only closed her eyes, and shook her head with the slightest motion.

Rukmini glanced at the house, then looked back at Arundhati. Ram cooed to himself in the backseat. The bangles sat in the palm of Arundhati's hand, a half century old, perfect rings gleaming yellow in the New England sun. Rukmini opened her handbag and took out a tissue. Then she wrapped the bangles, slowly, and put them inside her purse.

KARMA

Shankar Balareddy, unemployed professor and former convenience store clerk, and Prakash Balareddy, successful cardiologist, were as unlike each other as any two brothers could be. In the old Indian way, they lived together in a luxurious house in the Boston suburb of Lexington, with their respective wives. Yet the home was not entirely traditional—Prakash was the head of the household although Shankar was the older brother. Prakash owned the house and the car, and had a lucrative career. They had lived like this for almost a year before things changed one evening.

When Prakash came home from the hospital that night, Shankar had cooked a typically delicious meal: eggplant with peanut gravy, fish curry, and tomato *rasam*. Shankar's wife, Neha, put Prakash's son to sleep in the crib, and set the table with the second-best china. Prakash sat down at the dining table with the authority appropriate for the breadwinner of the household. Prakash's wife, Malini, complimented the food. Lady, the AKC-registered German shepherd, lay with her large head on her paws, content to be near them all.

But Shankar knew something was wrong. His brother did not look at him, although they sat directly across from each other. Prakash chewed fiercely and refolded his dinner napkin twice. His mood affected everyone around him; it had been that way since they were children. Dinner conversation dwindled, then stopped. When Prakash finally spoke, everyone flinched slightly, as if his voice were too loud.

"Shankar," Prakash said, looking at the food on his plate. He had long ago given up calling his older brother by the respectful title *Annaya*. "I have been thinking. I have decided that it is time for you to go from here. You and Neha should move into your own home."

"What?" Malini's head jerked up.

Neha stared at a candlestick on the table.

But Shankar met his brother's eye and looked at him slowly, full in the face, and blinked as if he did not understand.

"But he has only just lost his job," Malini said.

"He has been irresponsible," Prakash said. "How can he argue with someone at the convenience store when he is the checkout clerk? Who will come to the store afterwards? Perhaps one could excuse it, except that he was similarly rude to that customer in the taxi." Prakash wiped his mouth with his napkin. He cleared his throat and pushed back his chair.

"Besides," he said, addressing his brother, "I won't let you go just like that." Prakash snapped his fingers. "I will give you some money to start—five thousand dollars, shall we say?"

"Prakash! I don't agree!" Malini said.

"It will be good for you." Prakash spoke to his brother only.

"What about the baby? Who will take care of him?" Malini said. Neha glanced at her.

"I think you will learn how to live in this country," Prakash continued. He stretched his arms across the table, and his usually controlled voice grew animated. "How can you depend on me always? If you need support I will be here, but you should learn how to be independent."

"As you say, Prakash," Neha responded. Although she spoke softly, there was nothing meek in her voice.

Shankar could only look away. He suddenly felt very small. He was painfully aware of his brother's broad shoulders and long legs. Next to Prakash's clean-shaven, handsome face, his own moustache must have looked silly. Five thousand dollars to get rid of a brother! Economics—this was the way that the powerful always took advantage of the weak. Hadn't the British occupation of India started with one minor trading post in Surat?

The following day, Prakash retained a real estate agent to find Shankar an inexpensive place to live. The second day, a clean, one-bedroom apartment was leased in Arlington, in a redbrick building located on a street off Massachusetts Avenue. The real estate agent even managed to find a used sofa, eating table, and bed frame to furnish it.

On the third day, their suitcases, some old cooking utensils that Malini would not need, and the extra wooden chairs from the basement were loaded up in Prakash's Range Rover, and Shankar and Neha were deposited on the threshold of their new life.

*   *   *

Shankar was a graduate in colonial history from one of southern India's best universities. Then his brother, in deference to their dying mother's wishes, sponsored him for a green card application. Of course Shankar moved to the United States. Who would not, if given the opportunity? In Boston he had been a taxi driver, then a convenience store clerk, but in his heart of hearts, he wanted to be a chef. Today, the fourth day after his brother asked him to leave his home, he was none of those things. He waited in line to file a claim for unemployment insurance at the Massachusetts Division of Employment and Training office in downtown Boston, on the other side of Beacon Hill from the State House, behind a large man with a bald head and a double chin. From time to time the man looked around and shuffled his feet. Two women sat at desks in the front, helping the jobless. There were few people waiting behind Shankar: a dark-haired mother with a little girl, and a man with gray stubble on his chin who smelled of dried perspiration; he wore a shirt with his name on it—"Leo." How was it that everybody else in the city of Boston had a job?

Shankar heard a series of computer-generated beeps, then a woman's exclamation, then the banging of desk drawers.

"Can't believe these clerks." The bald man turned and looked down at Shankar from his height. "Wish they'd put in an honest day's work."

"Leo" took a few steps to the front and peered over the counter before returning to the line. The little girl tugged on her mother's arm impatiently.

"What's happened?" Shankar asked the large man.

"Computer's down. Second time this week. Now they've switched to the paper claims. I sometimes think they do it on

purpose so they can go home early. I'm not leaving, though."
He reached for the waistband of his jeans and pulled them
higher.

Shankar opened his mouth to say that the computer trouble
was no fault of the women, and that it was nice that they were
so willing to do the paper claims when the computer system
crashed. But the large man had bad breath, the kind that comes
from deep down, not just from failing to brush one's teeth.
So Shankar avoided the discussion and turned away to look
through the large panel of windows at the sunny May morning.

He could see the traffic on Cambridge Street: the cars and
men and women in suits hurrying to their offices, holding
paper cups filled with coffee. A dogwood tree was in blossom,
and the wind swept one white petal from a branch and carried
it away. Shankar imagined the petal in its flight past the stream
of cars, floating lazily in the spring sunshine, traveling to other
parts of the city under the perfect blue sky. What was he doing
in this line? What was his purpose? He wandered past the dark-
haired woman and her daughter, past the water fountain on
the left, through the glass doors into the chilly New England
morning sunlight.

He was familiar with downtown Boston because he and
Neha had traveled these roads with Prakash and Malini when
they first moved here. Since he left Prakash's home in Lexington, he had been trying not to think about that happier time.
Boston had been an adventure then. Now, looking at the same
streets, he was struck by the coldness of the residents, the
speed of their lives. He remembered the familiar warmth and
slowness of Hyderabad, the leisurely pace of people shuffling
by in *chappals* in the hot sun.

When Shankar was on Bowdoin Street, walking toward the State House, he saw a man sitting on the sidewalk. The man leaned against the cement wall of a building with his legs splayed wide and his bedroll beside him. He wore a frayed gray T-shirt and stared at a shoebox placed between his legs. A young woman dressed in a blue suit and high-heeled pumps walked by—a lawyer perhaps, or an executive from the Financial District, an aide from the State House. She stopped to talk to an acquaintance, a tall man with straight features and a newspaper tucked under his arm. When they said their good-byes she stepped back, onto the homeless man's shoebox.

From a short distance away, Shankar saw the scene unfold. The woman was startled; she tripped, then kicked the box again as she tried to regain her balance. The box turned over, spilling bills and change around the sidewalk. "Oh!" she called out. The homeless man did not react. With the patience of a child building sand castles at the beach, he placed his SOBER VETERAN sign next to him and picked up the money. The woman never met his eye. She did not put a coin in the box. She looked at him for only a moment, then she was on her way, adjusting her sunglasses, clutching her black briefcase to her side, the jacket of her suit swinging smartly behind her.

The unfairness of things! thought Shankar. The arrogance of those who have everything toward those who have nothing. He found two quarters in his pocket and crossed the road. He looked at the man's face as he stooped to put them in.

"God bless you," the man said.

Shankar smiled in response. He rose quickly and walked toward the State House and continued on, crossing Charles Street to reach the Public Garden. He sat on a bench next to the pond, watching the swans and the children who ran along the sidewalk. The sun was warm on his shoulders. Mothers walked past, pushing strollers. Business executives crowded the benches during lunch hour. The world was a sad, unjust place, he thought. It sometimes felt like an illusion; what was real existed under the surface of the blue sky and the green grass and the happy or tearful faces of children. He often did not understand why certain things happened to him, but he had always been able to rely on his family. Now, he could not do even that.

He had so many failures recently. His stomach turned when he remembered the argument in the convenience store. The man had been tall, about fifty years old. He wore a mono-grammed white shirt and a thin gold necklace. Shankar remem-bered that, because few men in America wore jewelry. The man had bought a can of Coke and a six-pack of beer, one of the more expensive brands. When Shankar told him the price, the man handed him a fifty-dollar bill. Shankar gave him the cor-rect change—he still remembered it was forty dollars and seven cents, but the man thought that Shankar was cheating him out of two dollars.

They quarreled. Shankar was humiliated. Did this man think him so cheap that he would steal two dollars? Did he look that desperate? Shankar raised his voice. He yelled. He felt the blood rushing to his head. The man asked him for his name and wrote it down on a piece of paper. He did not even ask Shankar to spell it. Shankar thought that was odd. He was fired the next day. When he thought about the incident, he was ashamed. Now, even his brother was fed up with him.

Did Prakash hate him now? Shankar's mind stretched back

to the long list of complaints that his brother had against him. They had not been truly friendly since they were boys, since their father died. Prakash had almost given up his medical education for Shankar, the older brother who could not focus on his studies. Their mother had said there was not enough money for them both to be in school. Prakash could not marry the first girl he had chosen because Shankar, unemployed even then, wasn't married yet. Tradition dictated that the older brother must marry first, and their mother always followed tradition. Perhaps Prakash was right: their mother had loved Shankar best.

When the sunshine no longer filtered through the willow trees, he asked a passerby what time it was. He jumped up to catch the subway to Harvard Square, and then a bus to Arlington.

Neha was waiting for him, watching TV. He could smell their dinner on the stove.

"I am sorry," he said. "I did not realize the time. It is the changing light. The days are so long now."

She got up and placed the rice and dal on the table. He put his hand on her shoulder, but she did not even look at him.

"Are you angry with me?" he asked in Telugu.

"No." She smiled.

"The computers were down at the unemployment office, so I did not file the claim. I did not find any work, either." He was glad to be able to speak to her openly.

"Everything will happen at the right time."

She served him before serving herself, rice and lentils, a bit of mango pickle—a modest meal, and easy to prepare in a kitchen that was not yet fully stocked. They sat at the small table, not looking at each other, but feeling that they were close.

It was at times like this, when Shankar felt that he had failed to provide Neha with the life she deserved, that he remembered the first time he saw her. It was at a temple on the outskirts of Hyderabad, when she rang the bell after her prayers. He was sitting, as he often did, on the low marble wall of the temple. Sometimes he would spend a whole day like that, observing people who walked past. He was at first struck by her beauty, which perhaps only he could see: she was dark-skinned and only five feet tall. But her eyes were gentle and lively and above all, kind, like those of the cows that wandered near the temple gate. She had brought a bag of sweets, which she gave to the children of the beggars sitting on the ground outside the wall.

He put his hand on hers as it lay in her lap.

When Neha finally spoke, it was in a low voice. "I have taken a job," she said softly.

Shankar took his hand away.

She stopped eating and leaned back in her chair, looking at him intently. Perhaps she was searching for hidden displeasure, but he had none for her. Was this not caused by his own deficiency?

"It is filling grocery bags at the market." She reached for him under the table. Shankar clasped her hand again, and squeezed it very tight, so that he would not lose her.

Lying in bed that night, he remembered something that had happened in his youth—a foolish act. He was walking in the forest with his brother when he saw two lovebirds on the branch of a tree, cooing and nuzzling in the shade. Because Prakash urged him to—there was no explanation for it other than that—Shankar aimed his sling and shot at them, and gave a yelp when one of the birds fell to the ground. Shankar was a religious man, and in his heart, he feared that Fate would visit the same destiny on him. He had not known that lovebirds mate for life.

When he woke in the morning, it was still dark, and there was an empty space in the bed beside him. He sat up with a jolt, thinking that Neha had already left, then he heard the water running in the bathroom. It was important to him to leave the house early: he must start his day at the same time she did.

It was the third morning that he had woken up in this room. Each morning, he had been newly disappointed. A battered wooden dresser and nightstand stood close by. The plaster had chipped from the ceiling in the far corner. The hot-water faucet in the bathroom sink spun around uselessly.

How different from Prakash's home, where the bathrooms gleamed and smelled like lemons. The walls were clean and white. The oak-wood floors always shone as if covered by a film of water. Even with Lady's thick German shepherd fur, the living room smelled only of the flowers that Malini put on the side table.

"Are you getting up so early?" Neha stood in the doorway, already dressed in her work clothes, her wet hair wrapped in a towel.

"I want to start early," Shankar said. "The line at the unemployment office was so slow."

"In that case, breakfast will be ready soon."

Shankar thought she was pleased.

The Star Market grocery store was open twenty-four hours a day and Neha's shift started at six. Neha and Shankar boarded the bus that traveled down Massachusetts Avenue, and Neha got off at Porter Square. Shankar continued on, then caught the subway at Harvard Square to the Park Street stop.

He had been full of hope when he waved good-bye to Neha from the bus, but when Shankar saw the homeless people on the Common, the sad, dreamy mood returned. The early-morning breeze swept plastic bags, cups, and debris through the streets. The sky was gray and heavy, the streets were empty, and a faint smell of urine hung in the air. He recognized the sober veteran lying on a bench near the fountain, with his shoebox under his head. Shankar stood in front of the closed door to the office of the Division of Employment and Training and heard a clock chime the half hour. Six-thirty. It would be two and a half hours until the office opened. Why had he not foreseen this? What was he doing here so early?

He had too many thoughts in his head, too many misgivings and too many questions to sit quietly and wait for the office to open. He turned and began to walk, and in two hours had traveled from Staniford Street to the North End, then to the Aquarium and to the Financial District. The streets began to fill with people. The walk had been good for him; his mind had cleared.

Then, in the shadow of the skyscraper at 100 Federal Street, he saw a bird. It was a still, olive-green spot on the sidewalk. If Shankar had not been looking down, directly at the place where it sat, he would have missed it altogether. He walked closer, until he was standing right next to it. The bird's eyes were closed and he realized that it was shivering slightly.

People with jobs scurried around him. A seagull circled overhead. A man in blue jeans brushed his shoulder. Shankar bent down on one knee and saw a pair of black pumps barely step clear of the tiny creature. The bird had black streaks on its wings, and its closed eyes were circled in white. The feathers were puffed outward, as if to protect itself. When Shankar drew near, it opened its eyes for a moment and closed them again, as if exhausted. The bird was comforted by his presence, Shankar imagined. It needed help.

He gently cupped his hand under the bird and lifted it up. It was unresisting, fragile; the tip of its beak was broken. He remembered the animal hospital where, three months ago, he and Prakash had taken Lady to have a tumor removed from her hind leg. The drive had been about forty minutes from Lexington. There had been a T stop close to the hospital—the ride could not be that long. There, this sad bird could get help.

Shankar walked back to the Common. The sober veteran had woken up, and was sitting on his bench with his bedroll and shoebox beside him. Shankar did not know if the man would recognize him from yesterday, but he reached inside his pocket and brought out a five-dollar bill.

"I'll give you this in exchange for your shoebox."

The fellow looked up at him from under the rim of his baseball cap. "I ain't a fool, boy. I got at least five dollars in there myself."

"Just the box. Take your money out and keep my five dollars."

The man looked at him suspiciously for a moment. Then he removed his baseball cap, emptied the contents of the box into it, and handed the box to Shankar.

Shankar put the bird inside, slowly. At the T stop he asked the man behind the counter for directions and boarded the train to Angell Memorial Animal Hospital.

*   *   *

Only two people were in the waiting room at the animal hospital. A man held a cage containing an orange-and-green parrot,
and an elderly woman sat with a small white Pomeranian on
her lap. Shankar waited with them for only a few moments. He
had told the receptionist that the bird needed help immediately,
and she had put him at the head of the line. Soon, a young man
led Shankar into the examination room.

The veterinarian was dressed in a white coat, like the one
Prakash wore at the hospital. When Shankar entered the room
he extended his hand. "Timothy Creswell," he said. He was a
slight man with a beard and blond-gray hair that was thinning
along his temples. His voice was so quiet, and his fingers so
gentle when he held the bird, that Shankar liked him immediately.

"What happened to this little fellow?" Creswell asked as he
lifted the bird out of the box. "Where did you find him?"

"On the sidewalk. In the middle of downtown. No trees
were nearby. I don't know why he would be there."

The veterinarian nodded. "This tiny guy is a ruby-crowned
kinglet. It was kind of you to bring him in, most people would
just walk by."

He peered into the bird's eyes and carefully spread the tiny
wings. He tipped the bird toward him and examined the head.
"There are no broken bones. That's good. They're very hard to
set in a bird this size."

Shankar stood by, his hands clasped behind his back. "His
beak is broken."

"We can fix that. We file it down and it grows back as easily
as a fingernail."

"He will live then?"

"Perhaps. He has eye damage. That may mean swelling in the brain, which can be fatal." Creswell went to a counter in the back of the room and returned with a small syringe. "This is dexamethasone." He picked up the bird, and it began to shiver again. He gently inserted the tiny needle into the bird's breast. "Steroid. It lowers the blood pressure so it reduces any swelling."

"When will we know if he will live?" Shankar asked.

"Probably by tomorrow."

"And doctor—" Shankar hesitated. "How should I pay for these services?"

"This type of case is usually handled by the wildlife rehabilitation clinic anyway. Let's just say it's on the house."

Shankar raised his eyebrows and smiled. "In that case, may I know how the bird is doing tomorrow?"

"Certainly. Tell Martha at the front desk. She'll make a note of it."

Shankar did not go back to the unemployment office. After leaving the animal hospital, he had the sudden desire to cook a delicious meal for his wife. On his way home he stopped at an Indian grocery store and bought a complete array of spices, some eggplant, and two types of bitter gourd. When he was finished, he had spent seventy-six dollars and ninety-five cents of the money that Prakash had given them. He thought that his day had gone well; he had saved a bird and stocked their new home with what he considered to be essentials.

When Neha returned, the bags of spices were sitting on the countertop and he was cutting the eggplant to soak in salted water. Neha's hair was falling out of its braid and her face glistened with perspiration. She collapsed into a chair in the kitchen.

"How did it go?" he asked in Telugu.

She told him about the young manager who had shown her around the store. A friendly college student was the checkout clerk in her aisle. She was not ashamed, she said, to have gotten this job.

"There will be a time when we do not have to do work like this," he said.

She shook her head, as if dismissing the thought. "And you?" she asked. "Did you file a claim?"

"No. But look—" He waved his hand at the spice-laden counter. "I've bought everything that we will need." He spoke enthusiastically, but he caught the glimmer of disappointment in Neha's face. She smiled at him anyway.

"That is good," she said. "It will feel more like a home now." She went to the bedroom to change her clothes.

He was chopping the onions when the phone rang. Neha answered it in the bedroom, and her voice was low and unclear. Someone from the new job, perhaps.

She appeared in the baggy pants and long shirt of a *chalwar kameez* outfit. She closed the bedroom door behind her. "Prakash is on the phone."

Shankar stopped chopping. Neither of them had mentioned his brother's name since they had moved out on Saturday.

"What does he want?"

"He said that we left some things there. A suitcase. He wants to know if we can pick it up." She was standing beyond the door to the kitchen, outside of the room.

"How? We don't have a car."

"Can't you come talk to him?"

"No. I won't." He shook his head.

"Shankar—"

"Tell him I am busy cooking." His voice grew louder. "Can't he drop it off? He is the one that has the car."

"There is a bus. He wants us to come tonight."

"How can he call today and command us to pick it up immediately? He is the one always talking about the American way of long-term planning." He was almost shouting now.

Neha was quiet.

"I will go tomorrow," he said finally. "Tell him that. Will you come with me?"

She nodded her head. "I will tell him that you will call before we come."

When she returned, she sat with her back to him at the far end of the sofa.

"You are upset?"

"Sometimes you scare me," she said. She did not turn to look at him.

"Because I am a failure."

"No. Because you are angry." Her face was half hidden at this angle, and the light from the window could not reach it. "You were never angry in India. Only after we came here. During the time we lived with Prakash you became more and more angry. You think everyone is against you, but you don't say anything back. When you do, it comes out like it did when you drove the taxi or worked in the convenience store. But people are not so bad, Shankar, the world is not such an unfair place."

"I have disappointed you."

"You have scared me." She turned and he could see her eyes. "What if you are rude like that to me someday?"

Shankar did not answer. He stood with the knife in his right hand, the left one poised over the onion. Suddenly he did not feel like cooking at all. He packed up the eggplant and onion and put them in the fridge, then took out the leftovers from the night before.

Neha was in the shower when he woke up the next morning. He thought immediately of the suitcase he had left behind. It was the blue one with the broken wheel. Even as he left Prakash's house on Saturday, and the luggage was piled in the back of the Range Rover, he knew the blue suitcase was not with the others. He had found some comfort in that; at the time, he had not wanted to go back into the house to get it.

The morning was gray and somber. From his bed, he could see only the thick cover of clouds that blocked out the sun. Today he would get a job, file for unemployment insurance, go and meet with his brother. Today he would set everything right.

He and Neha boarded the bus and parted at Porter Square, and he reached downtown at the same time as he had the day before. He was looking forward to the early-morning walk and the time it would give him to think. Neha was right. He should not be angry with anyone. He should only work to make their life better, then perhaps his brother would respect him as well. Helping oneself. Isn't that what Mahatma Gandhi taught? The philosophy eventually led to the British withdrawal from the subcontinent. He would begin living his own version of that philosophy today. He set a brisk pace for his walk and headed toward the ocean.

At 53 State Street, Exchange Place, he saw another bird. Before he could scoop it up, he saw another, lying on its side. Across the street, in front of the bank ATM machine, was a third. A seagull swooped down to the sidewalk and pecked at it. Shankar waved his arms and ran toward the gull, forgetting to look for cars on the road, chasing it until it flew off. That day, on the sidewalks of the Financial District, Shankar found eleven birds that were injured, and three that were close to death. He salvaged some paper bags from a trash can, poked air holes in them and placed the birds inside. In front of the Borders bookstore on School Street, he found a box to carry them all.

By the time the streets had filled with the working crowd, Shankar had forgotten about his resolutions for self-help, and Mahatma Gandhi, and Prakash's lack of respect for him. He found himself seated on the T, holding a box full of birds, heading for Angell Memorial Hospital once again.

"What do we have here?" Dr. Creswell asked, taking the box and putting it on the examination table.

"I found them all this morning. Early."

"Where?"

"Downtown. All along the streets. You would not imagine—there were so many! A seagull was trying to eat one and I chased it away."

Creswell slowly unwrapped a paper bag and took out the first bird. He spread its delicate wings and peered into its eyes. Next to this man, with his soft ways and his gentle hands, Shankar felt like a fool. How was this veterinarian so successful and yet so kind? His brother was not like that.

Creswell did not look up from his work. "Judging from the time of year it is, and the number of birds you've found, I think that these are 'tower kills.'"

Shankar stood with his hands behind his back, looking at him respectfully.

"Hundreds of birds die every year during the migration season, when they travel thousands of miles by night."

"Why?"

"It's still a mystery." Creswell put the bird down and made a notation on a clipboard. "The theory is that on cloudy evenings the birds are forced to fly low, under the cloud cover. They can't find the moon and stars. They lose their ability for celestial navigation and become disoriented. Whole flocks get confused when they see city lights. Some die quickly when they slam into the sides of buildings and towers. Some spiral slowly down into the lighted area, lose their way, and are trapped among the buildings when daylight returns."

"I have never heard of this," Shankar said. "Can we stop it?"

"The animal rights groups are trying to teach people. They say it's as simple as turning off the lights in the skyscrapers at night. I heard there's going to be a rally about it at the State House on Friday morning." Creswell had separated the birds into three groups on the examination table. He called into the back room for an assistant.

When the assistant entered, he stood next to Shankar, and Creswell summarized his findings for both of them. "There are fourteen in all. I will keep three overnight for observation, but I think that we can release them outside the city tomorrow. These six we'll treat here for now, but they'll go to Manomet tomorrow, to the wildlife rehab center. These"—he indicated the last group—"I'm sorry, but four of them have died. This little one is in very bad shape. I think that we will have to euthanize."

Shankar nodded his head slowly. "I have done some good, haven't I?"

"Absolutely. If you keep this up, we'll have to arrange for daily bird runs to the rehab center." Creswell smiled. "You really should attend that rally tomorrow. I know some people who would love to meet you."

"And the one that I dropped off yesterday?" Shankar asked. "What has happened to him?"

Creswell washed his hands in the basin. "His swelling was reduced. I'm sending him to the rehab center until his beak grows back. He'll be perfectly fine in a while." He turned to go, his hand on the doorknob.

"Dr. Creswell—"

"Yes?" The door was open; the veterinarian wanted to leave.

"I—"

"Would you like us to inform you of how these birds are doing?" Creswell asked.

"Yes, but—"

"But?"

"Would you have any jobs?" Shankar blurted out.

"Any jobs?" Dr. Creswell blinked.

"A job. Just one job. For me."

Creswell looked at him for a moment. He closed the door. "As a matter of fact, one of my ward attendants just broke her ankle, and won't be coming in for a while."

Shankar sucked in his breath.

"It's not glamorous work. Nine dollars an hour. Cleaning out the cages. Feeding the animals, taking their temperatures, timing when they take a poop."

"It sounds fantastic!"

Creswell smiled. "I've never heard it described that way before. The job is yours. Go upstairs to personnel and fill out the forms. Tell them to call me for information. Come in tomorrow and we'll start work."

Shankar clapped his hands once, loudly.

"I'm sorry. Did you tell me your name yesterday?" Creswell asked.

"Shankar Balareddy." He took Creswell's hand even though it was not extended, and shook it violently.

"Welcome to Angell Memorial, Shankar."

"I have found a job," Shankar declared to Neha that night, as soon as he walked in the door. She had her back to him as she was cooking at the stove.

Her jaw dropped open and she turned. "How? Where?" she asked in Telugu.

"I found a job! I found a job!" he sang to the tune of a popular Hindi song. He picked her up around the hips and spun her around the small living room.

"Put me down!" she screamed playfully, her long braid trailing behind.

He told her about everything: his early-morning walk, the birds, Dr. Creswell, his request for work. Neha leaned forward and listened. Her eyes were alive and her cheeks were flushed. He took her face in his hands and kissed her.

The phone rang.

"Don't answer it," he said.

"But it may be Prakash."

"That is why."

She got up and turned to look at the clock in the kitchen. "Shankar! The suitcase! Look at the time. The last bus leaves Harvard Square in ten minutes and we will miss it."

The phone rang again, then was silent.

"Let it be."

She bent down to look at him. "We promised."

"What promise?" Shankar stood suddenly. His wife backed away. "Did I promise to jump every time he calls? Did he keep any promises to me?"

Neha leaned against the wall. She spoke softly. "He kept the promise for one year. But now we must be on our own." She stepped forward slightly, pleading with him. "I do not want to live under his roof for my whole life. A combined family is good, but maybe not in America. How long would you keep me there?"

Shankar said nothing. He did not know that this was how she felt. He sat down slowly.

"I will get the suitcase tomorrow," he said, rubbing his eyes. "That is my promise to you, not to him. I will go straight from work, so that I will not miss the bus."

They sat down to dinner, but they didn't speak. He had found a job today, but he was not happy. His brother had separated them from each other, and he could not eat.

The next morning, he found ten birds. He put them each in a separate small paper bag that he had brought for the purpose, so that the darkness of the bag would calm the bird, and the bird would not harm itself if it struggled. Creswell examined each bird patiently. Only one had died, and another was euthanized. Again, Creswell told him to take part in the State House rally. So few had experienced the consequence of tower kills the way he had. Shankar shook his head. "Crowds of people. I will have to talk to strangers. It is not my type of thing."

Shankar learned to clean out the cages, and to feed each animal—ferrets, rabbits, dogs, cats, parrots—according to its weight. He learned to monitor when the patients ate and defecated, or behaved unusually, and how to record it on the "tin back" clipboards. He learned to cover his shoes when he went into the ward with the "Parvo dogs" and the "URI cats." He restrained a Saint Bernard in the examination room so that a vaccine could be administered. When all these duties were finished, he made heparin flushes—syringes filled with sodium chloride solution and heparin—for the surgery unit. He liked this duty the most, because it was done in Creswell's examination room, and they could talk between patient examinations.

"I have not seen such care for animals before. Cardiology unit and dialysis, even radiation therapy. In India, we do not have such things."

"We're lucky to have the best equipment available." Creswell wiped the examination table with a disinfectant. "But I would guess that Indians respect animals more, ultimately."

"In my old office we kept a nightingale in a cage who used to sing quite sweetly for us. But the dean believed that it was wrong. If we kept birds captive, he thought, we would ourselves be held captive in our next life. My mother used to have the same view."

"What did you do in that old office?"

"I was a professor of colonial history," Shankar said. He could feel the veterinarian looking at him. He laughed slightly. "Perhaps not a full professor, not yet. I was finishing my master's thesis. I was looking for a job when my brother thought I should come here. My visa number came up. He is a cardiologist." Shankar did not add more.

"Would you have come if it weren't for your brother?"

"I don't know. In America, I don't think there is a need for professors of colonial history." Shankar stared at the small syringe in his hand. "Sometimes, late at night when my wife is asleep, I think I will open my own restaurant."

"You're a chef, then."

"Just a dream. I do not have money like that. Only five thousand dollars that will soon be used in rent and groceries." He thought of his brother's house and the Range Rover and the diamond ring that Malini wore.

"Why not try the bank, maybe the Small Business Administration. That's what they're there for."

"I have seen the office downtown. I don't know if I am that kind of person." Shankar collected his box of syringes and prepared to go. "Such things seem like they are for dreamers."

"Exactly," Creswell said. He opened the door for him.

Shankar walked slowly to the surgery unit to deliver the syringes. Creswell had had an easy life, Shankar thought. He must have a lucky star guiding his path, like his brother, while his own surely fell from the sky years ago. He packed up his things to catch the bus to Lexington.

*   *   *

The bus ride was about a half hour, and took Shankar past the convenience store where he used to work. It had been only a week since he had seen this neighborhood, but it felt more like a year.

When Shankar rang the doorbell, his brother answered almost immediately. He was wearing tennis shorts and a matching shirt; his face and neck glistened with sweat. Shankar thought that he had been laughing just before he opened the door. When he saw Shankar, the smile disappeared. He held the door closed so that Shankar could not see inside.

"I thought you were coming yesterday," Prakash said.

"I couldn't."

"You should have called."

Shankar did not answer. He had not called on purpose, just to irritate his brother; but now that he had succeeded, he was ashamed.

"Won't you let me in, *Thumudu*?" he said, addressing his younger brother in the affectionate way.

Prakash looked back, over his shoulder. He opened the door a little wider, and Shankar stepped in.

"Wait here," he commanded. "I will get the suitcase."

Shankar stood in the shadow of the doorway in the foyer. He did not call out to see if Malini was there. He did not see Lady. From the foyer he could gaze through the panel of windows in the living room, and see the tennis court and backyard.

Three men were walking off the court. He recognized Ramesh Chundi, a wealthy businessman who used to live in Kansas. The other two players were not Indian. One was unfamiliar, but when Shankar saw the third one, he gasped.

"Who is that man?" he asked when his brother returned with the suitcase.

"Did he see you?"

"No."

Prakash hesitated. "He is my colleague, Jonathan Curtis. He wants to make me a partner this year."

"Did he tell you about me? In the store—did he recognize my last name?"

"He asked me if Balareddy was a common name in India. He told me what happened there," Prakash said.

"Is that why you thought it was time for Neha and me to leave?"

Their eyes met. Prakash did not answer. Had Shankar really believed that they could live together—in the old way—as their mother had wanted? Later Shankar would think that this silence was the worst response he could have received. It meant that Prakash knew the depth of his own betrayal.

"Does he know we are brothers?"

"No," Prakash said simply.

Prakash opened the door and Shankar stepped outside. The door shut behind him, and he was glad. He would not want Prakash to watch him struggle with the suitcase as he walked down the street.

Early the next morning, Shankar saw a small ruby-crowned kinglet fluttering against a window only a foot above the ground at 53 State Street. He scooped it up with both hands, and, seeing that it was only disoriented, he quickly put it in a paper bag. The bird was immediately calm. How odd, he thought. He had not yet seen a bird that was so confused but still managed to fly.

He was surprised to find no other birds that day, even though he walked the full daily route that he had created for himself. What did it mean? Had the migration stopped?

About a block and a half from the employment office, announcing its existence with large block letters, stood a storefront that Shankar had passed many times. He walked to it slowly, knowing he was going there, but not wanting to hurry. SMALL BUSINESS ADMINISTRATION, the sign said. He had not looked inside before. He closed the paper bag and put the kinglet down for a moment. He cupped his hands around his face and peered into the window. It was not like the unemployment office, where the counselors sat at desks with no barriers in between, and where each client could hear the complaints of the one seated next to him.

This office had cubicles and computers and guest chairs in each space. A coffeemaker stood in the corner. He had a strange thought that for the past year, only the storefront had existed; the desks and chairs and cubicles had magically appeared just as Dr. Creswell was telling him about it the day before.

The office opened at nine, but it was only eight. He would come back, he told himself. He turned to walk to the Common and the T stop.

A crowd of people had gathered at the State House steps. They held signs and led dogs on leashes. He walked to the top of the hill to watch for just a moment. He passed the homeless people on their benches, many of whom he now recognized. There was a hum of excitement, and two men were setting up a microphone on the sidewalk on Beacon Street. TURN OFF YOUR LIGHT! HELP THEIR FLIGHT! one sign said. SO LITTLE MEANS SO MUCH! said another. It was the rally that Dr. Creswell had mentioned, and Shankar watched the crowd intently for a few minutes. How fine it was that these people were here, he thought, even though he would not join them. Even though it was not his type of thing. The bird stirred in the paper bag as he walked back to the subway.

Devadasi

The November that Uma turned sixteen, her parents took her to India for the first time. Although she sat in her bedroom for a full day after her father announced the journey, although she protested the loss of eight days of school, the celebration of Thanksgiving, and her place in that season's *bharatha natyam* recital, even her mother did not give in. It would not look nice, Geeta said, if Uma missed the wedding of the daughter of her father's favorite cousin. Of course Uma's two brothers chose not to come; after all, they were in the middle of their medical residencies, and they were grown, and they were men. They could not be forced as she was.

It was 1992, the year that she had first noticed the graceful curve of her lower back, the firm roundness of the buttocks that the highschool boys wanted to cradle in their palms. It had been three years since her father had lost his vice president's position with Raytheon and become a mere consultant working out of his home. Two years since he had begun giving money to the VHP party in India, which sought to preserve the nation for the Hindus. He began to perform the Vedic ritual *pujas* at every festival and every season. It was Bhaskar's way to maintain self-respect after being "let go" following twenty years of loyalty and service, but Uma would not realize that until later. This is the way she would remember it years afterward, and she would not be entirely wrong: that she developed breasts, and her father became more Hindu; that she began to menstruate, and he thought it was time to take her to India.

Two weeks before, she had gone to a party at a classmate's home and drank beer with her friend Karl Harrison, a senior soccer player. In the back hallway he had kissed her face and neck and placed his tongue in her ear, and it felt like a feather had caressed the length of her spine. For months she had been wishing that just such a thing would happen.

She waited to tell him about her trip to India until the day before she left. "It's the middle of the year," he had said. He had a quiet way of speaking which invited intimacy. "Why are you going now?" She told him that it was her second cousin's wedding, and even as she was saying it, the answer embarrassed her.

"It's not like I want to, you know," she said quickly. "I've never even met her." But admitting that only made her feel more stupid.

"Just tell them you're not going," he said. But Indian girls didn't do such things.

Instead, Uma had struck a deal with her parents. In exchange for traveling to India, she would have private lessons with a very accomplished dancer that Amruta Auntie, her long-time Boston instructor, knew in Hyderabad. The dancer lived beyond the boundaries of the Muslim neighborhoods in the Old City, near the Nehru Zoological Park. Their driver would take her every other morning from her grandparents' home in Banjara Hills at seven forty-five, to return from the lesson in time for Geeta to do her wedding shopping at the jewelry and sari stores on Abid Road.

With this deal in mind, Uma packed her suitcases and boarded the plane with her parents before Thanksgiving, resigned to two weeks without Karl. They arrived in Hyderabad on a windy tropical morning twenty-two hours later, wearing the sweaters they put on in Boston, carrying bags that seemed much heavier now. Her grandfather hugged her awkwardly and her grandmother pinched her cheeks. Together they got in the leased car with the hired driver and made their way to Banjara Hills west of the city.

On the second night of her visit, they went to a dinner party at the home of Uma's grandmother's cousin, who lived with her son and his family. Their only child was Uma's age, and Uma had looked forward to the company of a teenager, but he had remained in his room, seeming mysterious and interesting because he never came to greet the guests. Two other families had been invited, and the women and girls gathered immediately in the back room, talking about jewelry and recipes and saris. Uma was wearing a crimson silk *schalwar kameez* that her mother had bought for her earlier in the day. She was feeling self-conscious; she had refused to wear the veil modestly over her breasts, draping the *dupatta* over her left shoulder instead. She forced herself to sit quietly on a stool in the corner of the room. A friend of her mother's stroked her hair. "Such a perfect maiden, Geeta," the woman said in Telugu. "Just we need a little dot, here, on the cheek, to take away the evil eye." Her mother showed her off—a straight-A student, a dancer who would have her solo *arangetram* performance that summer, a modern—but good—girl.

Uma rose and wandered out of the room, past the curtain which separated the teenage son's room from the hallway. Through a slit in the drape she saw him on the bed, his back propped against a pillow, a book resting on his thighs. A lamp on the bedside table threw a dim circle of light around him. How comfortable he was, how removed from the vapid chatter of the women. She wished she was in her own bedroom in Lexington, pehaps also reading a book, perhaps snuggled under her bedspread having a secret phone conversation with Karl. Then she remembered—it was Thanksgiving Day.

In the living room, the men sat with their scotch and sodas, talking politics. She heard their conversation before they noticed her. The talk was about the Barbri Masjid, the mosque in northern India that Muslim invaders built hundreds of years ago. The men were speaking of the hordes of Hindus who were gathering near the site, where ground would be broken for a new Hindu temple.

"What is the good they are doing there?" a voice rose above the others. "What will they accomplish by gathering? Someone will insult someone else, the Hindus will blame the Muslims, the Muslims will blame the Hindus, and just like that there will be *gudbud* in the streets. Communal rioting. Looting and killing."

"The authorities will never let that happen," Uma heard her father say.

"You have been out of the country too long, Bhaskar. You don't know."

"Shouldn't we Hindus be a little angry?" Bhaskar asked, then stated his reasons for why the Muslims should be sent to live in Pakistan: "They were foreigners who came five hundred years ago and forced the real Indians to convert or die. They weren't loyal to India despite benefitting from quotas in schools and jobs. They married three or four wives despite the population problem."

Uma heard his arguments many times at their dining table. She never understood why her father felt so passionately about people and places that mattered so little in his life.

She was an Amerian who did not care about the differences between Hindus and Muslims. She did not care about saris or Indian jewels, or that women should not be too familiar with the company of men. She walked past the living room to the covered verandah and sat down on a comfortable chair facing the garden. She did not know when she fell asleep. When her mother woke her, it was raining, and the driver was waiting for them in the gray-green Ambassador, idling just inside the gate.

Her parents did not know how much she loved to dance, which was fortunate for her. If they did know, they would not have approved. Just a generation ago, a young dancer would often leave the practice as soon as she acquired a husband, for it would not do for other men to look at her onstage, performing. In the old *old* days, the dancers were women of ill-repute, her mother told her—prostitutes who lived in the Hindu temples and were "married" to the deity. Despite this background, when Uma was six years old, her mother drove her to Amruta Auntie's house and she took her first class in the basement studio where so many other daughters of Indian parents learned to dance. How else, these parents thought, would these girls learn about their culture in a meaningful way?

The morning after the dinner party, Uma waited on the verandah of her grandparents' home for the ride to the first dance class. She sat with her mother at the breakfast table. Geeta was eating *sitaphul*, and a small piece of the fruit was smudged at the corner of her lip. Her mother seemed younger in India; she laughed easily and let her hair hang to her shoulders, and often explained to her relatives, unasked, about how things were in the United States.

The sun had risen in a cool sky over a clean city. An imam intoned his call to prayer. The vegetable vendors pushed their carts past the gate of the house, and no dust rose because of the moisture of the night before. Her mother leaned back in her chair when the kitchen servant came to clear away the plate of *sitaphul* skins. "How are things, Muthyam?" she said affectionately to the girl. "Are you well?" Muthyam wore a faded red sari with frayed edges that hung two inches above her bare feet. A small silver nose ring glimmered against her dark skin. Geeta had known the girl's mother when she was a child.

Muthyam smiled shyly without looking up. "All is well, *Amma*. Everyone is well," she whispered. She bent low, so that her head would not be higher than Geeta's, then left, taking the dirty plate with her.

She was a year or two younger than Uma, and this knowledge made Uma very uncomfortable. "So, do you like India?" her mother asked suddenly.

Uma could not answer. She had been to a dinner party; she had been shopping; she had driven past local landmarks. She did not have enough information to assess an entire country. *Do you like India?* She did not like their driver's furtive glances at her through the rearview mirror when she sat in the backseat. She did not like the experience of the day before, when, following her mother inside a sari store, a man had hung his tongue out at her hungrily. After they entered, the salesmen were too solicitous, groveling, piling each exquisite silk sari on top of another until they were ten or twelve deep. She and her mother stepped out of the store, holding two bags each. A young woman, dressed in a torn cotton sari, sat begging just outside, holding her baby to her breast. *Do you like India?* Perhaps her mother did not notice all these things.

"Why do the men always look at the girls here, and stare, as if they've never seen a girl before?" she asked.

"Are they bothering you?" Uma nodded. "They're just uneducated. They think you're different and well dressed, coming from a foreign country. They're unexposed to sophisticated things, that is all."

But some of those men had looked very educated to Uma. She thought of the students they had driven past on the medical college campus. They had seemed pampered and groomed; still the men had leaned forward to gawk at her inside the car. She suddenly wished she had worn her *dupatta* in the traditional way.

She did not say more to her mother. What was the point of arguing about everything?

The Ambassador roared up to the house. The driver got out of the car and, noticing Geeta, raised his hand to his chin in salaam. He seemed barely nineteen.

"Hello, Hafeez," her mother said.

He was not handsome, Uma thought. By American standards, he would have been considered ugly. His face was all angles, cheekbones and jawline and fluffy hair that sat loosely on his head. She had noticed for the past three days that he had worn a type of uniform: a clean but dingy, untucked button-down shirt, polyester pants, leather open-toed *chappals*. His prominent wrist bone was visible as he held the steering wheel or shifted gears. He was nothing like Karl, whose soccer jerseys draped his shoulders perfectly, as if he were a mannequin.

Her mother spoke to Hafeez in Hindi, and then looked at her for a moment. Uma could understand only a little of it, but she knew that her mother was telling him once again where the teacher's home was. Geeta had talked to the dance instructor three times on the phone since they had arrived. The instructor had made it clear there was no reason for Uma's mother to come to the first class.

Uma climbed into the backseat of the car. She stayed on the left-hand side, so that Hafeez could not see her through the rearview mirror, then felt annoyed at herself. Why should his gaze bother her? Karl had looked at her like that on the strange day before she left for India, and it had not bothered her then.

Uma waved at her mother as the car pulled out of the driveway. She was suddenly aware of being alone with the driver, but they did not speak. The windows were open and the morning air played against her face as they sped through the easy wide roads in Banjara Hills, then met the heavy traffic in the city. Now and then a cow or goat ambled across the road. Car horns blared, joining with the honks of the auto rickshaws and scooters, the sharp bells of the bicycles. They stopped at a traffic light and she felt the dull thuds as cyclists grabbed onto the outside of the Ambassador, steadying themselves. The smell of exhaust invaded the car's interior. Hafeez seemed focused on negotiating through traffic. Sometimes he yelled in Urdu out the window.

They traveled past the pale stately buildings of Osmania General Hospital, then across the Nayapul bridge, where the lush greenery lined the banks of the Musi River. The stone structure of the Hyderabad High Court lay on the other side; suddenly they were on an older street with elegant buildings in the Muslim style. They reached the intersection that framed the four stone towers of the Charminar. Here, almost all the women were draped in black burkas and the men wore white prayer caps, their eyes rimmed with kohl. They were beautiful, Uma thought, in a way that the Hindu men were not. Their faces were structured and hard, while the Hindu men looked soft and fleshy. Suddenly, she was in a different place; why did an accomplished *bharatha natyam* dance instructor live far from the affluent Hindus, beyond the Muslim section of town?

The Ambassador stopped. Hafeez turned toward her, but not completely; she could only see the side of his face. "I'll take one minute," he said in Telugu. She did not know that he spoke the language. "Why?" she asked, but he was already gone. He had not stopped yesterday in this manner—unasked, without explanation—when she was with her mother and aunt.

Uma rolled up her window. Now a few people started to gather: some beggar boys tapped on the glass and pointed to their mouths, two men stood outside a storefront chewing pawn, a vegetable vendor gawked just a few feet from the car. A group of women shrouded in burkas walked past, holding books. The boys were becoming aggressive, knocking on the windows even louder, and a few others joined them. It was as if India were trying to get inside the car: the rude men, the beggar children, the veiled ladies who must think she was "loose." She was annoyed with Hafeez now, and just when she was starting to grow alarmed, he appeared and opened the car door, holding something white and soft in his hands. A strand of flowers.

"Jasmine, *Amma*," he said in Telugu, smiling, glancing at her. "They were selling it this *morning*," he said, as if it were unusual. He pointed with his bony finger. He had been only a few feet away, always in view, but she had not seen him. "The car will smell nice." He looped the strand over the rearview mirror.

It was true. The flowers transformed the interior of the Ambassador, as if the two of them, Hafeez and Uma, were floating in a fragrant bubble through the middle of the city. "I didn't know that you speak Telugu," Uma said. Her own command of the language was not good. She hoped he would not laugh. Then she wondered if a girl of her status should care if he laughed. She did not like the image of herself that he must see.

"Urdu is my first language," he said. "Of course I understand Hindi. Then I speak Telugu. Also I understand a little English and Tamil."

"I speak Telugu badly," she said. The remark was inappropriate—it was too familiar. He was silent.

He brought the car to a stop at the gate of a large white house. Red bougainvillea cascaded from the roof. Several species of palm lined the surrounding wall. She began to get out of the car when Hafeez said, "Just wait one minute here." He knocked on the front door and spoke with a young man who appeared there. Only then did he return to the car, step to the side, and open the door for her.

The dancer's living room was filled with sunlight that shone through the grids on the windows and patterned the floor at Uma's feet. She sat in an uncomfortable wicker chair and looked around at the old books and curios: miniature replicas of the Eiffel Tower and Big Ben, a snow globe of the Statue of Liberty. A red and orange silk rug covered the marble floor. A pair of *tabla* drums sat in the corner. There were no depictions of Hindu gods except a foyer statue of Lord Nataraja, posing in his dance of the cosmos, encircled in flame. The young man who had greeted her had disappeared behind a curtain at the far end of the room.

Uma waited for only two minutes when a woman pushed aside that same curtain. She was about forty years old, had a single long braid and wore a *chalwar kameez* that was the color of saffron. She wore no jewelry except a small pendant and necklace. Her skin was not as fair-complexioned as it appeared in many promotional photos, and she was so short that Uma could see over the top of her head. But her eyes were large and expressive, as a dancer's should be.

"Come," she said, and Uma rose and followed her up some stairs to a room with a large mirror that covered one wall. The same young man who opened the door was sitting on a floor mat.

"Raju will provide the *nattuvangam* for the lesson," the dancer said in Telugu.

Uma looked at Raju, who smiled respectfully. "Okay," she said in English, wondering why the teacher would feel the need to explain. During dance instruction someone always sang the rhythmic syllables and tapped out the beat on the wooden block; in Boston it was usually Amruta Auntie herself.

"You would rather speak in English?" the woman said.

Uma felt self-conscious. "As you wish, Guru-ji," she said in Telugu. Amruta Auntie had told her that this would be the proper form of address to use, but she felt that the dancer would laugh at her; it sounded so antiquated and formal. But the instructor merely seated herself on a mat near Raju and gazed at her. Uma felt exposed in the open space of the dance room, seeing her image in the mirror.

"So, you want to learn a dance to perform at your *aranget-ram*?" the dancer asked in Telugu. Her voice was small and low, and she pronounced her consonants precisely.

"Yes," Uma said. "In July."

"Amruta-ji told me to teach you *varnam*. It is a bit advanced. Usually pupils learn it earlier in their studies, so they have sufficient time to perfect it."

There was no smile. Just a statement.

"Amruta Auntie wanted me to learn as much as I could from you. I will practice very hard here, and on my own too, after I go back."

The teacher did not acknowledge her. "I must find out at what level you are dancing. Can you show me now? You must know *allaripu*."

Uma froze. She had danced *allaripu* years ago, but she

could not recall even the first motion of the dance. She laughed a small, embarrassed laugh. She stared at the teacher's face, not knowing what to do.

The dancer seemed to sense this. "Come," she said, and her voice was not unkind. "We will do just a few small movements first." She rose, but before beginning to dance, Uma watched as she gave the greeting so familiar to her from Amruta Auntie's classes: Guru-ji put her palms together above her head in salute to God, then at her heart in deference to her fellows, then at the floor to ask forgiveness of the Earth for stomping on her. Only then did she gesture to Raju to begin. He picked up the wooden stick and tapped out the beat, and his voice sang out the rhythmic syllables:

> *Tha te te theum, ki ra tha ka*
> *Tha te te theum, ki ra tha ka*
> *tham te tham te thut the*
> *tham te tham te thut the.*

The dancer stood up straight, barefoot, and brought her arms to shoulder level and bent her elbows. Her eyes, as dark and lovely as a deer's, moved from side to side in time with the rhythm; her head echoed the motion. Uma stepped forward and assumed the pose, following Guru-ji through the movements. The dancer's right foot crossed behind the left one. She stamped out a rhythm that echoed Raju's voice. Then Uma's legs and hands and feet remembered, and she began to dance.

The room was transformed. Uma saw herself in the mirror, and in the bend of her waist and the curve of her eyebrows, there was beauty. Her arms swept the room; her palms met to invoke the blessings of Lord Ganesha. Her feet and body matched every syllable that Raju delivered to them, and she felt herself command the space and air of the studio. The glances of the men on the street, the furtive look of Hafeez the day before, the tongue that hung out of the man's mouth at the sari store—they were gone.

"Very good," Guru-ji said, and Raju ended his chant. She nodded at Uma, and Uma saw herself in the mirror, gazing back at her, out of breath and flushed. For the first time since arriving in India, Uma felt free.

Uma had seen Karl Harrison the day before she came to India. They had been standing in the hallway in school after lunch, with two periods left until the end of the day. She had suggested they leave; he told her there was no one at his house, and it was so easy—just a thirty-minute walk, taking the shortcuts through the neighborhood backyards.

The sun shone brightly without real warmth, but the air was not cold. They walked in silence past the school grounds and left the busy streets. He had a newspaper tucked under his arm; he would often carry one and talk about a person's civic duty to vote. He had an older brother who had died from a drug overdose when Karl was only ten. He had another brother who had gone to Yale. All these things made him seem knowing and mature and sad and were things that Uma loved about him, although she couldn't have explained it; his world did not revolve around money and medical school. That day, the angle of the sunlight, the dying trees, the brisk air, the autumn melancholy—all of it seemed natural and therefore lovely and innocent to her.

He let them inside his house and immediately she felt the emptiness of it, the still space inside, and it was both exhilarating and frightening to her. In his bedroom, it was the same. The shaft of sunlight shone through the window to illuminate a square section of floor; they laughed as the cat batted the floating particles of dust. They were safe and alone and they took off their clothes slowly. He was slim, attractive in a way that never would have appeared in the magazines. He looked at her, and she welcomed the gaze, his attention slowly moving to every limb and curve, like a meditation. He did not insist, which made her want him all the more. But at the crucial moment she said no. She did not know why. In twenty-four hours, she would be on a plane to India.

He lay beside her, and she said, "I'm sorry." She did not realize that he had truly forgiven her until afterwards, when they were dressed, and leaving the house, and he took her hand as they walked to the town center.

She replayed that moment many times in her mind, that moment that she said no. It puzzled her.

The next time she went to the *bharatha natyam* class, Guru-ji smiled at her. It happened after Uma showed off the first portion of the dance that she practiced in her grandparents' home. Uma did not want to tell her how hard she had worked on the segment—three hours each of the two days, observing herself in the narrow, slightly distorted mirror that leaned against the wall of her grandparents' bedroom. The mirror was not even large enough to reflect the full range of her movements. But she felt such contentment while learning the new piece.

She had argued with her mother about having enough time

to practice. She had managed to escape a visit to a jewelry store in order to do so. Then, she found that her work on the dance sustained her during the shopping trips, and the two dinners she attended in relatives' homes. While riding in the car with her family, listening as they talked with shopkeepers, visiting the homes of relatives, the rhythm of Raju's *nattuvangam* stayed with her, and she could feel her body move to it even as she sat quietly on a shop stool or in a living room with older women.

In the car, on the way home, she said to Hafeez in Telugu, "It would be nice if Guru-ji lived closer to home."

"They like to live here," Hafeez said.

She wondered what made him say that, then remembered that she had seen Hafeez talking with a man who served as Guru-ji's driver; they seemed to be on friendly terms.

"Why?" she asked.

"Her husband is a Muslim. He is Usted Mohammed Ali Khan, the *tabla* master." Everything made sense, then, the lack of Hindu gods in the house, a home in a mixed area beyond the Old City. She realized how little she knew of what was possible in India. She thought of her parents, who shared the same religion and caste, whose marriage had been orchestrated by relatives. They were together because everyone around them thought they should be together.

By the fourth class, Uma had learned half of the dance—perhaps not the poetry and nuance of it, but enough to keep step with Guru-ji as Raju chanted the rhythm. After Uma had rehearsed it several times, Guru-ji sent Raju to fetch some water, and they drank slowly out of the stainless steel cups, catching their breath. It was warm in the room despite the early hour.

"Amruta-ji has many students in her school?" Guru-ji asked,

glancing at Uma as if she were truly interested, and not just making conversation.

"About two hundred. Small girls and older dancers, along with some Americans."

"So many." She raised her eyebrows. "And Americans want to learn too."

"Yes," Uma said, not knowing if it was a question or a statement. There was something she wanted to ask this Indian dance instructor, but she did not know how. With Amruta Auntie, it had somehow seemed an improper subject.

"Guru-ji, *bharatha natyam* is an old dance form, isn't it?"

The dancer was about to turn back to the instruction; she had put down her cup and moved to the front of the room. "Ancient. More than four thousand years."

"I heard that in the old days, the dancers would be 'married' to the deities at the temple. But actually . . ." Uma hesitated. She was vaguely aware of Raju standing just outside the room. "They could be with any man of the village."

Guru-ji smiled almost imperceptibly. "Who has told you this?"

Uma did not want to admit that it was her mother. "Many people believe it, don't they?"

"Yes, many people believe it." Guru-ji sat on a stool positioned just in front of the mirror, which reflected the single long braid of her hair. She was so quiet that Uma thought she would not speak again. But she sighed and said, "Mostly it is the British version of the story. When they came to India, they did not like the temple dancers, who gave their lives to the worship of God. They did not understand the religious nature of the performance. After all, we were just pagans to them."

There was feeling in her small voice—not anger, but something just as strong. "The British were not aware of the years of spiritual study and formal education that came with performing the dance. They arrived with their missionaries and their wives and daughters, whose behavior was so timid and docile. Naturally the missionaries suggested that the dancers were prostitutes."

Uma nodded. She had not expected such a full explanation.

"In the old days, Uma"—it was the first time the teacher had addressed her by name—"the dancers were the most educated women in the country. We had access to the kings and ministers, to the most powerful men. We did not marry, but we had our livelihood and our independence." Guru-ji looked at her as if to gauge her reaction. "Of course, many people do not know this. They see who the *devadasis* are now, the poor prostitutes, and believe that was who the professional dancers were in those ancient days." She rose and indicated that it was time for the lesson to resume. "You must study the history. Then, you must believe what your own mind and heart tell you is correct. Isn't that true of so many things."

It was not a question. Uma nodded again. She had never heard an Indian woman say such a thing before.

When the wedding finally arrived, Uma was tired of it. She had already met members of her extended family many times at the pre-wedding dinners and ceremonies. She wanted to stay home with her grandfather, who had a cold and excused himself from attending. Instead, she dressed in a fine silk sari and sat in the front seat of the car with her father, while the older women sat in the back. Hafeez left them at the entrance to the wedding hall, then turned the car to join the others waiting on the long driveway.

A large sign said SUNITA WEDS RAVI. Inside she saw the bride and groom sitting under the flowered shelter of the *mandap*, the bride modestly keeping her head bent low under the veil, her eyes focused on her lap. The brahmin continued his chant of Sanskrit slokas, oblivious to the guests milling about and talking in groups of men or women. Uma had heard there would be eight hundred attendees. Her parents and aunt and grandmother had already found their friends and cousins.

Most of the women in the family were seated on the stage near the *mandap*, ready to help if the bride should need it. Two of her aunts gestured to her to come and join them, and she smiled back, indicating that she would come in a few minutes. She did not intend to. There was a great burst of music, the *sonnayi* wailed loudly; the groom stood to tie the *mangalasutram* around the bride's neck. She watched the bride and groom walk around the sacred fire. The bride's veil was slightly askew, and a woman moved forward to fix it.

Uma noticed two young men watching her from the far side of the room. They were twins, eighteen-year-old sons of her mother's cousin, tall and big-boned and handsome. She had met them at a family dinner about five days ago. They had not spoken to her then, though she had tried to talk with them. She focused on the *mandap* for a moment, then glanced back. One of the boys continued to stare, and she moved behind a pillar so he could not see her. She thought of Karl, of how she would be with him soon. Nothing that had happened in India would matter then. The guests started moving toward their dinner tents, the men to one and the women to the other. Uma felt her mood sink.

She was glad to see her mother walking toward her, holding another woman's hand. "Here she is, Rohini," Geeta said, putting her arm around Uma's shoulder.

"Very pretty, Geeta," the woman said.

"Rohini Auntie was my childhood friend from before intermediate level."

Rohini Auntie smiled at Uma. Her mother beamed.

"Before you know it, everyone will be asking about you." Rohini Auntie moved her eyebrows up and down and smiled.

Her mother pulled her closer. "We don't want to lose her so soon!"

"Perhaps she will go to medical college, so you have a few more years," Rohini Auntie said. "You know my Deepa is in medicine."

Geeta responded in a soft voice, but still Uma could hear—certainly her mother meant for her to hear—"But let us know if you hear of anyone good. I mean anyone worth following for the next few years."

Uma looked away. As soon as her mother's hand slipped off her shoulder, she concocted a reason to go, and left the two women gossiping together. She hoped that they thought she was rude.

Outside, the air felt refreshingly cool. Three women sat on chairs near the entrance to the hall. A group of men huddled in the dim glow of the decorative lights, smoking and drinking. Their laughter drifted up into the night, above the tops of the *ashoka* trees surrounding the wedding hall. A line of cars stretched down the driveway with some of the drivers talking nearby. A collection of motorcycles and scooters, standing at various angles, blocked the sidewalk.

It was a beautiful night; beyond the reach of the lights she could see the full moon shining in a halo of silver, its glow reflected on the bumpers of the cars and motorcycles. Tiny jasmine blooms dotted the bushes decorating the compound, and their scent wafted through the air, reminding her of the first ride alone with Hafeez twelve days ago.

He was standing there now, smoking a cigarette, and talking to someone behind the gate, just beyond her line of vision. As Uma came closer, she saw that it was a young woman in a dark burka. She had thrown back her facial cloth, exposing her teen-aged features. Her lips were crimson, and when she brushed a strand of hair away from her forehead, Uma saw that her hands were decorated with henna and that the fingernails were tipped with red polish. She was lovely, and she angled her face toward Hafeez with an easy smile and a sense of familiarity.

Uma was surprised that she felt jealous. By the time she approached Hafeez, the girl had moved on and joined some others who were walking down the street. When Hafeez saw her, he dropped his cigarette, snuffed it out under his *chappal*, and touched his chin in salaam.

"Who is that?" Uma asked in Telugu.

Hafeez looked shy. "She lives in my neighborhood, just three houses from me," he said. "A friend of my sister's. She is attending a wedding just a short way from here." He clasped his hands behind his back. "My mother also just walked past. She is attending the wedding too."

Suddenly it seemed that his was the only friendly face she had seen all evening, even though she had spent three hours in a large room crowded with relatives. She opened the back door of the car and sat down, her legs hanging out the side. "There are so many weddings tonight!" she said. "It must be an auspicious date." But then she remembered that the other wedding would be Muslim; both faiths would not calculate an auspicious date in the same way.

Hafeez hovered in the vicinity of the car. He unclasped his hands, then played a rhythm on the hood, then leaned against the side, then straightened himself. "Please sit, Hafeez," she said. "I am waiting for the others. I grew tired of the wedding."

Hafeez seemed startled, but he opened the door on the driver's seat and sat down sideways, just as Uma was seated in the back. "There are so many weddings tonight," she repeated. "Tell me who is getting married in that other one," she said, and they talked about the groom, whom Hafeez had known since childhood. Uma asked if Hafeez would have gone too, if he had been free this evening, and he said that he would have. He asked about Christian weddings in the United States and Uma spoke about them with authority, even though she had never been to one. Hafeez turned on his radio to a station with songs from the Hindi cinemas. *Ek ladki ko dekha to aisa laga jaisay khilta gulab jaisay, chandini rath, jaisay mandir mein ho jalta diya.* "I saw a girl who looked like a blossoming rose, like a moonlit night, like a prayer flame in a temple." The Bollywood music blocked out the sounds of the party; they could no longer hear the chattering women or the laughing men. The songs drifted from the car's speakers, past the tops of the *ashoka* trees into the darkness.

Half an hour passed before Uma saw her parents and her grandmother and aunt emerge. Rohini Auntie was with them, and a man Uma did not know, presumably Rohini Auntie's husband. She and Hafeez were still talking with the car doors open, leaning sideways on their respective seats, Hafeez slumped and at ease. That was how her parents and their friends found them: Uma in a gold-threaded sari the color of flame, Hafeez in his loose shirt and pants, sitting together in the Ambassador, as if they were equals.

"Uma!" her mother said. Hafeez jumped to his feet.

"Uma," her father repeated, with more authority. "We have been looking for you."

She knew instantly that they were very angry, and she knew too that they would try to hide it, because Rohini and her husband were there, and the most they could do for appearances' sake was to pretend that nothing irregular had happened. She rose slowly from her seat.

Rohini Auntie and her husband said good-bye. Hafeez quietly took his place behind the steering wheel. Uma turned to get in the car and walked to the front, where she had sat with her father earlier in the evening. But he stopped her. "Get in the back." He indicated the direction with his chin. The implication was clear: the front seat was too close to Hafeez, the front seat was where, from now on, only he would sit.

She looked at her father.

"Get in the back," he repeated.

"I will not," she said.

"Uma," her mother called. "Get in the backseat, young lady, with us."

Uma did not move.

Her mother leaned out of the car. "Right now."

The radio hummed in the background. Uma stared at her

mother. Her heart was beating very fast when she climbed into the backseat and sat down.

"When in Rome, do as the Romans do," her father said cheerfully from the front, as if the good-natured tone of his words would hide the reality of what had happened.

On the way to Banjara Hills, the radio program was interrupted to give an update of the latest news; the Barbri mosque in Ayodhya had been destroyed by a militant Hindu mob, using sledgehammers and their bare hands. No officials from the Indian government or the police force had attempted to stop them. Four of the men had been trampled during the demolition, and at least a hundred were injured. Widespread Hindu-Muslim violence was expected in that region. Uma thought she saw, on her father's face, a small twist of a smile.

The next morning was her last dance class. Uma woke and looked out the window of her room and saw that Hafeez had arrived early; his car was parked in the usual place. The anger of the previous night descended on her like a cloud. She dressed quickly and went downstairs. She heard her mother's voice in the kitchen, talking with the cook. She had no wish to see or speak to her family today. She gathered up her bag and went outside to the car.

"Even today you are going to the lesson?" Hafeez asked. He never would have asked her in that way, unless they had talked with such familiarity the night before.

"Yes. Why not?"

"We shouldn't go to the Old City. Because of the Ayodhya issue, they have called for a *bandh* and the stores have closed.

Only the government offices are open now. I am sure there will be a curfew."

"I don't care," she spat out in English. She wanted only to escape to the dance studio. "It doesn't matter," she said more calmly, in Telugu. "What can happen?"

"Does sahib know that we're going?"

She felt a flicker of anger. Why was it is his concern if her father knew? "Yes," she lied.

Traffic was lighter than usual, but Abids did not seem different this morning. It was only after they crossed the bridge that Uma noticed few men on the streets, and no women at all. In the alleys, metal doors were clamped down on the entrances to shops and hotels. A handful of vegetable vendors stood in the shadow of the Charminar. There was an air of expectancy; only the cows and goats seemed to saunter about without a concern. She noticed the change but said nothing.

A few moments later they turned onto a familiar side road. A barricade had been erected several hundred yards away. Hafeez braked and swept the car around to retrace their path.

When Uma noticed the men, they were still far off and scattered, and she didn't recognize them for what they were. Then she realized that they advanced together, separately but coordinated, like the muscles in a snake's body. She felt a shudder in the car's engine, as if Hafeez's foot had faltered on the clutch.

"Remove your *bindi*," Hafeez commanded, pointing to his forehead. There was an unfamiliar tenseness in his voice. He was looking at her through the rearview mirror.

She stared back at him, not understanding.

Hafeez turned and looked at her directly for the first time. His face seemed angry. "Remove your *bindi*," he said again.

She tore the sticker off her forehead. And then something happened, something that had been programmed in her for years, perhaps since the day she was born, when her parents knew she was a girl-child. She picked up the *dupatta* on her shoulder and veiled herself, putting the cloth around her head and neck and breasts, so that only her face was revealed.

The men gathered around the car, surrounding it so that it couldn't travel farther, and Hafeez slowly rolled down the window.

"Where are you going?" a man said. Uma knew enough Urdu to understand. The man carried a walking stick and wore a tight short-sleeved undershirt. A *dhoti* was tied around his hips. From her seat in the car, Uma could see his dark, brittle calves.

Hafeez gave Guru-ji's address in the Old City. "The home of Usted Mohammed Ali Khan," he added.

"Who is she?" The man pointed to the backseat with his chin.

"His cousin-sister. She comes from abroad."

The man bent down and looked into the window. Uma was alarmed at the beauty of his eyes, the Muslim handsomeness of his face. His eyes were rimmed with kohl, and he stared at her slowly, his eyes traveling from her face to her breasts to her stomach. She felt anger rise up in her, and it was familiar; it was connected to the wedding of the night before and the way she had been brought on this trip to India. She had been stupid to think that she was American, that differences between Hindus and Muslims, men and women, meant nothing to her. She had been stupid to think that she could sleep with Karl.

She bent her head under the *dupatta,* and fixed her gaze on the hem as it lay on her lap. She knew the man with beautiful eyes was considering what Hafeez had said. She heard him speak to another standing beside him. Her future was being discussed—back and forth between two men, and a third yelled his opinion from the back of the crowd. What would happen if they told her to get out of the car? Then she heard a laugh—low and guttural. She did not know who it was.

When the man spoke again, he was standing upright.

"*Challo,*" he said, motioning to Hafeez to leave.

Hafeez put his hand on the gearshift. The man with beautiful eyes yelled at the crowd and the others moved aside. The Ambassador edged forward slowly. At the end of the street, Hafeez turned the car toward her grandparents' home in Banjara Hills.

She looked up and saw her face in the rearview mirror. It was pale, filled with relief and another emotion she could not identify, or even remember feeling before. The Ambassador began to speed through the empty city streets. She realized she was trembling. Hafeez gripped the steering wheel with both hands and his knuckles were white. Guru-ji would be wondering where she was, and Uma pictured her teacher standing in the dance studio, alone, waiting. Her eyes stung. For a moment, Hafeez looked at her and then looked away, and she felt a surge of despair about her place at home and in the world.

LORD KRISHNA

Krishna Chander was fourteen years old when his family moved from Cambridge, Massachusetts, where his mother could buy a decent sari at a store in a certain neighborhood, to Wichita, Kansas, where there were only twenty-six Indian families in all, and only one, other than his own, that spoke Telugu. His parents enrolled him in the best private school in town—there were only two—but that didn't stop some members of the football team from sometimes calling him "towel head" when the teachers weren't around, or his classmates' parents from complimenting his English, or the prettiest girls in class, from the oldest Wichita families, from just ignoring him. It was 1981, after all. The Iran hostage crisis had just ended, Ronald Reagan was in power, and India was a Third World blip on a map, just a notion that had faded away with the hippies.

Krishna muddled along, hanging out with his only real friend, Linus Wong, taking care to avoid the Graber twins and Big Jed

Khoury and Laura Travis, who was sometimes seen holding her nose when he was near. Then came the day in American history when Mr. Gabriel Hoffman, history teacher and minister in the Church of Christ, brought in some pictures of the devil. Linus wasn't in class because of a doctor's appointment, and, to make things worse, Krishna had been forced to take the only vacant seat, between Harlan Graber and Big Jed.

Krishna was lucky; Harlan wasn't paying attention to him. Instead, Harlan was sitting behind Joe Hamilton and rapping the back of Joe's head with his knuckles. Joe whipped his fist back to hit Harlan in the calf and snapped, "Cut it out!" Harlan mimicked him in a girly voice, "Cut it out cut it out," as Big Jed chuckled.

But as soon as class began, Krishna's luck ran out. Harlan started making blowfish faces at Krishna while Mr. Hoffman wrote on the blackboard, and Krishna determined that he would say something, and finally the words "stop it" slipped out of him in a small voice. Some of the other guys snickered, which made Hoffman turn around to ask, "Is there something going on that I should know about?"

"No."

"Nothing."

"No, sir."

The answers came from boys sitting in all different corners of the room, but still Mr. Hoffman stared hard at Harlan and then at Krishna, as if Krishna were the cause of the problem. He was a smallish man with a slight paunch, thick glasses, and a bald spot that he tried to cover with a comb-over, and he never understood how much the kids made fun of him. Still, Krishna didn't like to be caught in that stare; his mother had taught him to always respect his elders, and his father believed that one should be the center of attention only when one excelled at something in a magnificent way.

Mr. Hoffman resumed his lecture on John Brown and the defense of the City of Lawrence, and talked about the Free-state men and the Wakarusa War. About the time that he asked the students to turn to page one hundred and twenty-nine in their text, Toke Graber raised his hand and drawled, "Hey, Mr. Hoffman, weren't we going to talk about the devil today?"

The students looked up with more interest than they had at any other time during the lesson, and Krishna felt a pang of admiration for Toke. The truth was that Krishna longed to have the bravado that these boys had to run down a football field as easily as they did, or dribble a basketball, or drink beer, or talk to girls. He hadn't felt this yearning with his Cambridge friends, who never cared that he was shy. Their parents had visited India in the sixties. They listened to Ravi Shankar and ate spicy food and sometimes burned incense in their homes.

"Hey, Mr. Hoffman, you didn't forget about it, did you?" Harlan asked. Everyone knew he was referring to the conversation they had in class previously, after a guest minister had delivered a sermon about the devil at Friday worship. "Satan, man." Toke beat a rhythm on his desk. "What about the devil?" other students called out, and some of the girls joined in, even Margaret Williams, who was black and always sat shyly in the back of the room. Mr. Hoffman had developed a reputation among the students; they knew they could divert his attention for a long time simply by asking any question about religion. That fall, they had already discussed how Jesus would have handled the Iran hostage crisis and whether the world had been created by God or the Big Bang. Two weeks ago, Mr. Hoffman had presented his view, aligned with that of Tertullian, that women should not address the students and faculty gathered during Friday-morning worship. No one participated in that debate very much, especially not the girls. Krishna would sit and listen to these discussions, and sometimes he would sit and *not* listen to them, and even more seldom, he would sit and consider if heaven and hell and God the father and Christ the son were really how things were.

But no matter what his reaction, he always felt that he was looking through a large window at people in a parallel world, one that was familiar but that he didn't understand. Krishna could know these people, look through that window and wave to them, but he would never be one of them. His father explained that Americans lived their lives in one way, and their own family lived in a different way. There was nothing very similar between them. Americans didn't even love their children as much as Indians loved theirs. Krishna didn't know if this was true, but his father believed it enough for the both of them, and he never thought to question it.

"I haven't forgotten the follow-up discussion we were going to have on the devil," Hoffman said. "And I did bring some examples of satanic influence that we mentioned last time." He pointed at a small suitcase sitting under the blackboard. "But it's a very serious discussion and I didn't want to mention it again unless the class really wants to hear what I have to say."

The students begged and pleaded and played their part. Finally, Hoffman muttered something about the importance of their spiritual lives and the salvation of their souls, and wrote NEW TESTAMENT REFERENCES TO SATAN in huge letters on the blackboard. Underneath, he listed several verses. Krishna could feel his mind drifting away to the cloudy November day that he saw through the classroom windows. The first-graders were being let out for recess, and a tumbleweed swept across the green stretch of the tennis courts outside.

"Get thee behind me, Satan!" Mr. Hoffman bellowed flinging his arms out wide. Krishna started. "That's what Jesus Christ said to the devil on the mountain." Hoffman was glaring at them through his thick glasses, his eyes looming large. The students shifted in their chairs; few of them knew how his congregation admired him at the Church of Christ on Great Plains Street. He had organized a trip for five missionaries to evangelize Cameroon, Africa, and he had created a television program, *The Power of Prayer!,* which was broadcast every Sunday in Kansas, Missouri, Nebraska, and Oklahoma.

"There's no doubt that Satan exists," Hoffman said, "and that he is the master of lies and deception. The Bible refers to him as a real entity." Hoffman pointed to the list on the blackboard. "But Satan is a genius. He knows that young people would never purposely follow the devil, they must be tricked into it. What's the way to trick someone into following Satan?" He looked around the room, then lowered his voice. "Make them believe that Satan doesn't exist." The clock on the wall ticked ominously. Krishna heard Mr. Hoffman's slow footsteps on the hard floor.

"Because if Satan doesn't really exist," Hoffman's voice boomed again, "if he's merely a marketing tool used by slick advertising executives, then all the books, music, and games that celebrate him can't really be that bad, right?"

Krishna glanced at his classmates. They were listening with

attention. There was something different about Mr. Hoffman now. For once, he seemed to know something important. His voice was deeper, his speech more sure; he had grown six inches in a few moments.

"But the Bible states that Satan is as real as you or I. He makes you yell at your parents, or causes your brother to crash his car. He's at work when a drunk man beats his wife, or when a healthy person hears voices, or when a five-year-old boy, like that poor child on the west side, jumps off a balcony to his death."

There was a collective intake of breath; everyone had heard about that boy. For a moment, Krishna was alarmed. Did Hoffman believe that Satan was real in that way—that he whispered in a child's ear and made him jump? Krishna felt the hair on his neck rise.

"That's the genius of Satan. By convincing mankind that he does not exist, he makes himself more and more powerful." Hoffman set the suitcase on his desk and opened it. With a flourish he held up a thin, oversize book—the Fiend Folio from Dungeons and Dragons. "Notice the ways in which Satan insinuates himself into what many people think are just innocent games," he said, handing the book to a student to pass around. The teenagers glanced at each other, disbelieving. Some faint snickers and muffled snorts swept through the class, like a breeze rustling a field of wheat. Even six-foot-three, pot-growing Larry Hook cracked a smile. Krishna grinned, too, feeling a sudden, quiet kinship with them all. Mr. Hoffman's spell was broken.

But the teacher didn't notice. He reached inside the suitcase and pulled out more things: a Ouija board, a three-volume edition of *The Lord of the Rings*, newspaper clippings about goth fashion, a magazine article about the New Age movement, a church-published pamphlet about voodoo. There were album covers by Black Sabbath, Iron Maiden, Judas Priest, AC/DC, and a poster of *The Blizzard of Ozz*, with Ozzy Osbourne sporting a reptilian tail and red cape.

Harlan cleared his throat. "This is all very interesting, Mr. Hoffman."

"More than interesting, Harlan," Hoffman said. "Integral to your salvation!"

The clock on the wall said they had two minutes remaining when Harlan handed Krishna the glossy page torn out of a magazine. The illustration was of azure-hued, smiling Lord Krishna in his classic pose, wearing his crown with a peacock feather, one leg crossed in front of the other, his flute to his lips. The same picture hung in the sitting room of Krishna's grandfather's home in Hyderabad; he'd seen it last summer. "I am the utmost devotee of Lord Krishna," his grandfather had announced, putting his arm around his grandson. "I was named for him, just like yourself. He is the most beloved deity in our religion." Krishna turned the glossy page over to look at the back. A tiny inscription read: "Krishna Consciousness, path to the Godhead." On the side were two frayed segments where the page had been torn from binding staples.

Krishna felt a chill. He looked around at the other students and his history teacher and his face flushed with embarrassment. Did anyone know what this illustration meant to his family?

The bell rang, and the kids hurried out, leaving the clippings and album covers scattered at their seats. But Krishna remained at his desk. He knew what he should do, and he knew what he was capable of, and they weren't the same thing at all. Krishna had long recognized his biggest flaws—he didn't stick up for himself, he was too skinny, and he was not cool in any way, except his skill in Donkey Kong. He imagined asking Hoffman where he got the magazine clipping, or politely informing him who the figure in the illustration was, or telling him he shouldn't have brought the picture to class.

But Krishna didn't do any of that. He just told himself he was looking through a large window at other people in another world. What they did couldn't affect him. He laid the page on Hoffman's desk and slipped out the door. Kids swept past on both sides, and the hallway opened before him without end, as if he were dreaming. The realization came to him slowly, clearly, as he dialed the combination on his locker. His teacher had known exactly what he was doing. Mr. Hoffman wanted Krishna to know he was going to hell.

Krishna's mother, Sarojini, was ten minutes late picking him up from school that day. She had just visited the only Indian grocery store in town, and the Hindu owner, originally from Gujarat, had informed her that he was closing it down for good. She had spent some time trying to convince him to stay open, or to sell to the Pakistani Muslim man who was interested. "Definitely I will close the store altogether rather than sell to *him*," the owner had replied. She had left the shop completely distraught.

In the car, Krishna tried to talk to her about it, then about Gopal Uncle coming to visit for Thanksgiving, but he kept seeing his own fingers holding the magazine clipping of Lord Krishna. Finally his mother asked, "What is wrong, Krishu?"

and he said, "Nothing." Only he wasn't very convincing, because his mother frowned and said, "Don't lie, Krishu. Good
boys don't lie." But he didn't think he was lying. Not really.
And at fourteen, he didn't think he was a boy, either.

At home, he changed out of his uniform, put on his jeans,
and walked the five minutes to Linus Wong's house. He didn't
know if what Mr. Hoffman had done was *wrong*, but he was
mad at Hoffman for bringing the picture to class. He was mad
at everything and everyone, he realized. Mad at himself for not
saying something to Hoffman afterwards, mad at his mother for
trying to cheer him up, but most of all he was mad that he lived
in Wichita, and there was only one person to blame for that—
his father. He was mad at the way his father never talked about
it with him, as if moving away from his Cambridge friends and
his cousins and his Gopal Uncle were the easiest thing in the
world.

Linus answered the door, smiling broadly, and Krishna was
mad at him for the smile. He thought about telling him what
had happened, but his friend shoved a large cardboard box into
his arms, saying, "Hey—my grandfather sent me the Meteor
airplane model," with a lilt that meant "I got it before you,"
and Krishna didn't want to tell him after all. Telling him would
acknowledge that they were both weird in some way. Already
he and Linus were the odd ones; they never dragged Douglas
Street with older kids on a Friday night, hadn't gone to homecoming, and neither of them had ever spoken a word to Laura
Travis, the prettiest girl in their class. He looked around the
Wongs' house and suddenly despised the jade dragons sitting
on the mantel and the furniture decorated with the mother-of-
pearl inlays.

"Why does your mother put all this Chinese shit in the house?" he said.

"Why does your mother put all that Indian shit in your house?" Linus said.

"Don't ask me," Krishna spat back. He hated her, and his father too, for just a moment.

"Who cares about the stupid house," Linus said, opening the box on the dining table. "Will you look at the wings on this thing, Krish?"

Krish, Krishna thought, as Linus fiddled with the wooden pieces. Krish Kris. Suddenly, that window that he had been looking through was turning into a doorway—one that he could step through, leaving behind these troubles that separated him from the other kids. He would start speaking up for himself, he thought. He would start tonight. He had a vague sense that it would make his father very angry. For the first time in his life, Krishna wanted to do just that. *Krish Kris Chris Christ.* He sat down to look at the new plane.

The family usually ate dinner in the alcove off of the kitchen, and that night they had chicken that Sarojini had prepared in their own tandoor. Krishna finished his second piece, licked his fingers, took a large gulp of water, and announced softly, "I want to change my name."

Ramesh Chander prided himself on his competence and self-possession. Upon hearing his son's words, he calmly folded his hands in his lap. "Who has put this thought in your head?" he said, not yet recognizing the immensity of Krishna's change of heart.

"I decided on my own." Krishna jutted out his chin. Something about the gesture made Ramesh angrier than he might have been otherwise. He never expected such boldness from his own son, who he sometimes thought was too mild-mannered, too observant of rules to be successful in life.

"I knew something was wrong today." Sarojini sighed. "Did something happen at school?"

"No." Krishna shook his head slightly, then shrugged. "'Krishna' is too hard to say. It's old-fashioned." He glanced at Ramesh, then back at his plate. "Tomorrow, I'm going to tell everyone at school to start calling me Kris. Spelled with a 'K.'"

"Kris?" Ramesh blurted. "What kind of name is Kris? You want to become like a local person or something?"

"Something must have happened at school, right, Krishna?" Sarojini asked again.

"What can happen at school?" Ramesh said. "Don't blame his nonsense on the school, Sarojini. You are always making some excuse for him."

Sarojini frowned.

"It's not about the school. It's about my *name*, okay?" Krishna said quietly. "I'll decide what people call me." He rose, put his plate in the sink, and walked upstairs. Despite his anger, Ramesh was impressed by his son's composure.

"I forbid you to change your name, Krishna," he called out.

There was no answer.

"Krishna!" Ramesh shouted, but the only response was the soft click of his son's bedroom door closing.

"Why must you scream and shout like that?" Sarojini said, slapping her napkin on the table and picking up the plates. "He won't listen that way."

"If you stopped supporting his ideas all the time, maybe that would help." But he knew that his wife wasn't responsible.

"Asking if something's wrong does not mean I'm supporting his ideas," Sarojini said.

"What is it then? Something bothers him at school so it's okay to forget his heritage?"

"I did not say that, Ramesh."

"Absolutely nothing is wrong with the academy. Half the students went to Ivy League colleges last year," Ramesh said, but he knew he was exaggerating.

"And the other half believe Jesus Christ helped them buy their car or cut their toenails."

"You encourage him to hate the school."

"Don't talk nonsense, Ramesh." Sarojini began to rinse the dishes at the sink. "He hates it all by himself."

For a few moments, there was only the sound of running water and the clink of plates being placed in the dishwasher. "My brother says that his business is doing very very well in Boston," she said finally.

Ramesh held his head in his hands, his fingers nestled in his thick crop of hair. Gopal had been asking him to start a joint business venture ever since Ramesh had left MIT. But he knew that if they moved back to Boston, their house wouldn't be as big, or his car as new, and his son couldn't go to the best school in town. He knew Sarojini loved all the Indian jewels she was able to buy with the success of his Wichita business. "How many times must I tell you?" he said. "The client is here, Boeing is here, so the business is here."

"You could carry on long-distance from Boston."

"You want me to be running, traveling here and there all

the time?" He wished he was in his office, where everybody listened to him, and the clients always seemed pleased, and his employees always acted cheerful. "We are not moving back."

"Gopal says there's a good market for your software there, and you could keep the contacts with Boeing here. Together you two could be minting money."

"We are not moving."

"Ramesh, there are more of our people there." She stared at him, nostrils quivering, while the water from the faucet gushed. "You know how much Krishna likes his Gopal Uncle, and he would have his cousins and his old—"

"We are not moving back to Boston," he said, loud and angry this time, turning his chair to glare at her. "He has to learn how to become more comfortable here. Do you think that always he'll have everything handed to him? There are some Indians in Wichita. Let him make friends with them." He turned away again.

"Some father you are, Ramesh!" She slapped the kitchen towel on the counter. "Dragging your wife and son around the country to satisfy your ego." She said these last words—"satisfy your ego"—with her eyes wide and her finger pointing at him with each syllable. "Forget about Boston, maybe we should be moving back home instead!"

"Don't be ridiculous!" he shouted, then realized she had said it only to taunt him, because as soon as the words were out of her mouth, she was marching upstairs. Sarojini loved Western-style comfort too much to move back to Hyderabad. He heard their bedroom door shut with a bang.

Ramesh got up slowly. He retrieved the week's issue of *India Abroad* and collapsed in his favorite armchair in the living room.

The house was quiet. The newspaper's front-page headline announced: "One Dead, Three Injured in November 3rd Kashmir Shooting." He had an odd sense that the house was empty, even though his wife and only child were just upstairs. He opened the paper. *Satisfy your ego.* "Central government officials believe shootings in Srinagar are related to recent Muslim militant activity to *satisfy your ego.* Prime Minister Indira Gandhi, addressing the Lok Sabha, accused the Pakistani government of violating the territorial integrity of India to *satisfy your ego.*"

"Bah!" he said, springing from his chair and throwing the newspaper on the table.

He went upstairs even though it was half an hour before his customary ten forty-five bedtime, and saw the thin band of light underneath his son's closed bedroom door. Just as Ramesh's feet hit the top of the stairs, the light went off. He hesitated and knocked softly. Without waiting to be invited, he turned the knob.

"Krishna?"

There was a pause, then Krishna's voice came from the darkness. "Yeah."

Ramesh walked across the room toward the bed. He hit his little toe against a hard corner and yelped as the pain shot into his foot.

Krishna sat up. "Are you okay?"

Ramesh hobbled to the bed and sat next to him, rubbing the area around his toe. "Fine," he gasped. It was not often that he came into his son's room. Usually, he just knocked on his door to wake him in the morning.

"Sorry," Krishna said. "I shouldn't have moved that table there. I was working on a new model."

"I don't know why you'd rather play around with toys than come up in my real plane with me," Ramesh said, then was immediately sorry. He shook his head, displeased with himself. "Yes, I do know why. It's because your father likes real planes, and you like model planes." He tried to keep the regret out of his voice.

They sat there for a while in awkward silence. It felt different with just the two of them, sitting in the shadows; usually Sarojini hovered around the fringes, helping them understand each other. Slowly, Krishna's face emerged as Ramesh's eyes adjusted to the darkness: the severe cheekbones, the skinny neck, that *quietness*. His son would never be handsome, not like he was.

"School is okay? You like your classes this year?"

Krishna shrugged. "They're all right. The math teacher's pretty nice. English is stupid as usual." He traced a line with his finger on his bedspread. "I wish we had a chess team."

"Right." Ramesh nodded. "Like in Cambridge." But he never understood his son's interest in that game. "That boy—Harold or Howard—is he still bullying everyone?"

"Yesterday he asked me where my turban was. As if we were Sikhs or Muslims or something." Krishna snorted. "He's such a jerk."

"There's no lack of those for the rest of our lives. Just wait, Krishna. In ten years he'll be a gas station attendant and you'll be filling up your red Porsche at his shop."

"He'll be a loan shark or something."

"Gas station attendant. Your father knows, he's seen it happen."

Krishna laughed a little. "Lamborghini."

"Okay okay, Lamborghini."

"Yellow."

"Yellow," he agreed. It wasn't so hard, Ramesh thought, doing this without Sarojini. They sat together a little while. Krishna's little laugh had eased the discomfort between them.

Ramesh picked up the model on the table and examined it. "It's quite good, this little plane. Technically correct, you know. Yaw." He moved the model in the appropriate angle. "Pitch."

"It flies real well. Me and Linus tried it out last weekend."

Ramesh put the plane down and nodded. "You should try going up again with me sometime. The second time is not so scary. Not like the first. It would be nice."

Krishna was quiet, and Ramesh didn't feel like talking about the name change. Not when it was so late. Not when they were actually getting along for a few moments, sitting together in the darkness. "Good night, Krishna," Ramesh said, leaning over to give Krishna—something; in the last instant, he realized it was a hug.

Tears came to Krishna's eyes, but he blinked them back. "Dad?"

"Yeah." Ramesh was already at the door.

"Something weird happened in my American history class today."

"Weird?"

"Mr. Hoffman brought in a picture of Krishna—the real Krishna—and told us it was satanic."

"He did what?" Ramesh said, his hand hanging limply on the doorknob, his eyes narrowed.

Krishna told him the story, and with each sentence, it seemed the burden was shifting, floating off the boy's shoulders and settling on the man's.

"How can they hire someone like that?" Ramesh said.

"Dad—"

"Did you tell him that he was an idiot?"

"He's my teacher."

"Did you tell him that he can't just insult your religion in that way?"

Krishna said nothing. Ramesh felt a surge of disappointment. When he had been fourteen, nobody could have spoken against him or his family without Ramesh setting him right. He sat down again on the bed. "That idiot teacher can't get away with that stuff," he whispered, staring out into the darkness, his shoulders slumped, his hands clenched into fists.

Only then did Krishna begin to fear what he had done. He had wanted only understanding—a quiet pat on the hand and some agreement that people were stupid. He should have known that his father, who had been a first-class student, who had been captain of his school cricket team, who had had no less than fourteen proposals for the arrangement of his marriage, who had been *cool*, would never tolerate this situation.

"I'm going to talk to the dean about this," Ramesh said. "What's his name? Marshall, Mackerel?"

"I don't want you to talk to Dean Mitchel."

"Krishna, sometimes you have to stand up for yourself," Ramesh said, springing from the bed. He could fix this situation in less than twenty-four hours.

"Everyone will make fun of me."

"No one will make fun of you. The other boys don't even need to know."

"I just want to forget about the whole thing. I won't even change my name, okay?" There was pleading in Krishna's voice now, a tone that made Ramesh cringe. He almost wished that his son would insist on changing his name; at least it would show determination.

"You can't let these people get away with this behavior. Tomorrow we'll have a meeting with him. Get yourself ready."

Krishna sighed, put his arms across his folded knees and lay his forehead on them. He had trusted his father enough to tell him what had happened, but his father had stolen the situation. I had become *his* insult, *his* experience, to be dealt with in *his* own competent way. When Ramesh left the room, Krishna was still sitting that way, even though Ramesh had wished him good night.

Ramesh walked slowly to his bedroom, distraught. A tiny thorn of regret pricked the back of his mind. Perhaps Sarojini was right after all. But he could not accept that, and he reminded himself of key bits of information: he was a self-made millionaire; he belonged to the second most exclusive country club in town; he lived in the same neighborhood as Henry Stone, president of Stone Industries, a Fortune 500 company. Why hadn't all this money protected his family?

He opened his bedroom door quietly, but Sarojini was awake, lying in bed, flipping through a magazine. She glanced at him when he entered, and he felt a twinge of embarrassment that he pushed away, and told her, very matter-of-factly, what had happened in Krishna's history class.

"That bastard teacher," he said, trying a light laugh. "Can't believe it. I want you to schedule a meeting tomorrow afternoon, Sarojini. With the dean, me, you, and Krishna." He counted the names on his fingers. "If Mitchel wants that bloody history teacher there, tell him to invite him. I want to look him in the eye." He turned over and snapped off the lamp.

Sarojini felt a wave of sadness wash over her. She knew the sensation well; it would overwhelm everything—her fury against Mr. Hoffman, even the hurtful knowledge that Krishna had chosen to confide in his father instead of her. It would take her days to break to the surface of the wave and breathe happily again. She closed her eyes and saw a familiar vision. On a map of the world, she was a black dot in the middle of North America, and her brother was another dot at the edge of the same continent. Half a world away, on a triangle jutting into an ocean, on a patch of earth filled with red dust and rice paddies and banyan trees, lay a cluster of black dots: grandmothers and aunts and ancestors who would have appeared on her map hundreds and hundreds of years ago, before the British, before even the Moguls had arrived. She opened her eyes again, and they were moist.

Dean Jonathan Mitchel's office had a round table placed next to his desk and a large window that looked out to the western edge of the campus, which sat on the outskirts of town. From the window, one could see the football field extending to the Johnsons' quarter horse ranch, the wheat fields farther on, then the silver grain silos behind which the sun set in November. It was the end of the school day; still the dean greeted the Chanders with a respectful smile and showed them to seats around the table. Krishna cringed when he saw his father's tan hand clasp the dean's freckled one; he sensed the meeting was really between these two men, and that he and his mother were extraneous. He felt very stupid and small.

"The last time we saw each other was in the ice cream line at the Blue Angels show at the air base," Mitchel said easily, in a Kansas twang. "My boy, John, was with me."

"Of course, I remember," Ramesh said, and Sarojini managed a smile, but Krishna sat with his shoulders slumped forward, hands tucked under his thighs.

"Mr. Hoffman will be joining us too," the dean announced. "When there's been a problem in a class, I always like to have the teacher here to answer for it." Krishna felt a churning in his stomach; he had not expected to see the teacher again so soon and in such close quarters. The dean talked about his excellent grades and his recent performance on the school's hi-Q team, and his mother smiled at him proudly, but he could not smile back.

Finally, they heard a light knock, and Hoffman stood at the door. "Sorry I'm late," he said. "A student kept me after my last class."

Krishna felt the sudden chill in his gut that he had felt the day before.

"Come in, Gabriel." Dean Mitchel frowned. "We've been waiting for you."

Krishna noticed his father stare at Mr. Hoffman, assessing him, while the teacher said hello and sat down.

"I have the utmost respect for this school, gentlemen," Ramesh began. "I send my son here because of its excellent academic standards."

"Ninety-eight percent of our graduating class proceeded to a four-year college last year," said Mitchel.

"I'm not here to talk about academics," Ramesh said.

"*We* are not here," corrected Sarojini.

"That's right. As you both may know, we're not Christians. This is a private school with Christian leanings—"

"The only thing we ask is that all students attend the service on Fridays," Hoffman said, looking at Mitchel, but Mitchel gave him no sign of acknowledgment.

"And the only thing *we* ask is that our culture and religion be respected," Ramesh said. He was smiling as he did when he was disgusted with something, looking directly at the teacher, one side of his mouth curled up aggressively.

"I don't follow you, Mr. Chander," Mitchel said, leaning forward.

"My son told me last night that you, Mr. Hoffman, had brought a picture of the Hindu incarnation of Lord Krishna to class yesterday." Mr. Hoffman glanced at Krishna, and Krishna breathed deeply. Why did his father have to say it as if Krishna had given away a secret? "He said you told the students it was a picture of the devil—something like that?" His father was trying very hard to control his temper; Krishna had heard him rehearse the speech that morning.

Mr. Mitchel's eyebrows rose a half inch, and he leaned back in his chair.

"I did bring in some illustrations yesterday," Hoffman stuttered. "Along with several record albums and books and some games. All things you wouldn't want your son interested in, I assure you. The students were curious about them because a guest minister recently spoke about negative influences in our lives. I didn't want to miss the opportunity to educate them in a positive way." Hoffman cleared his throat. "Which particular illustration are you talking about?" he asked.

Krishna opened his mouth and a small sound slipped out.

His mother and the dean glanced at him. This was his chance to redeem himself, to have the courage to speak up. Surely, his father should allow him to describe the picture; he was the one who had seen it. But his father didn't notice him at all. Instead, Ramesh described the illustration of Lord Krishna as if he had held it in his own hands.

The teacher's expression suddenly focused. "I know the one you're talking about!" He nodded his head. "But I didn't realize— I had no idea it was a Hindu concept."

They heard the drone of a fighter jet outside, listened to it approach, then fade into a distant sky. The three adults and Krishna looked at Hoffman. Krishna felt the teacher was lying. Yet Mr. Hoffman's eyes were wide, and two lines had appeared upon his forehead, as if he really were surprised.

"Not a Hindu *concept*, Mr. Hoffman," Ramesh said slowly. "A picture of a Hindu *deity*." Krishna was newly embarrassed. All this talk about gods and goddesses was what made Christians think Hindus were so primitive. But his father was continuing, making things worse. "And now my son, named in honor of his grandfather, who is also named for the deity, wants to change his name." Krishna felt his face go red. How stupid his behavior seemed when explained in that way.

"I *don't* want to change my name—not anymore," Krishna said, but nobody heard him, not even his mother. She had laid her hand on his father's arm, to calm him. She didn't like it when he lost his temper in front of local people.

Hoffman looked at the dean. "Let me explain," he said.

"Yes, why don't you," Mitchel said.

"I didn't realize what that picture was," Hoffman said. "One of my parishioners brought it to my church a month ago. She found it in a magazine published by the Hare Krishnas." He glanced at the dean, then looked again at Ramesh. "I wouldn't purposely insult you or your son, Mr. Chander. Everybody has their own religious beliefs. I can talk to the students about the importance of being a Christian in my own life, but I can't force anything on people." He looked around the table. "I apologize for not being sensitive to the effect it might have on your son."

"Do you mean to tell me that you don't know the difference between that silly American cult and the Hindu religion, which is thousands of years old? That's unbelievable," Ramesh said, shaking his head, but Krishna thought it was the most believable thing in the world. "Why don't you educate yourself? You call yourself a history teacher. These are the lies you teach in your class?"

Hoffman began to stutter again. "As I said, Mr. Chander, the students seemed interested, and I didn't want to lose an opportunity to—"

"To waste class time indoctrinating them in your religion?"

"Ramesh," Sarojini said.

The dean spoke up. "I can understand your concerns, Mr. Chander." He looked at the teacher. "I'm worried about this, Gabriel. It's an important matter. We run an accredited institution and we operate under certain objective criteria. The amount of class time spent on certain core subjects is one of them."

"I think that you should bring this issue up to the board," Ramesh said quietly. "And I think Mr. Hoffman should be fired."

Krishna did not like the expression on his father's face. Everyone knew that Ramesh Chander's company had donated ten thousand dollars to the school that summer, over and above Krishna's tuition.

"I'll talk with the board," Dean Mitchel said. "I'll inform you of their decision in a few days."

"I think that's appropriate," Ramesh said, and the dean nodded at him. In that brief exchange, Krishna felt that something very wrong had happened.

Hoffman looked at the people sitting around the table and swallowed calmly, but only Krishna noticed that his hands, folded together on his lap, were trembling. Hoffman seemed to have shrunk; he was as helpless as Krishna was when Harlan called him "towel head" while other students laughed. For a moment, Krishna loathed him. Then, Krishna saw him through that familiar window, through the glass that separated him from American life, and he sensed, for once, how to step through it. He knew he'd been mistaken; it had nothing to do with changing his name at all.

"I accept your apology, Mr. Hoffman," Krishna said, his heart beating in his throat. He had never contradicted his father, however softly, in front of others. His mother and the dean looked at him as if hearing him for the first time, but Ramesh didn't react at all; Krishna didn't know if his father had even noticed him speak.

Krishna was not certain why he said it. He knew only that Mr. Hoffman's eyes met his, and for a second, he thought they understood each other. He wasn't sure that Mr. Hoffman apologized sincerely. For years afterwards, even after he went back to Boston for college, Krishna would struggle with his memory of the exact meaning of Hoffman's words. But in that moment, accepting the teacher's apology was the only thing he wanted to do.

"Thank you, Krishna," Mr. Hoffman said, holding his gaze, and the ice in Krishna's stomach melted away. It suddenly didn't matter that Krishna had never wanted this meeting at all.

The adults were quiet for a moment longer than usual. "I'll follow up on this situation and get back to you, Mr. Chander," Dean Mitchel said.

"Please do." Ramesh stood abruptly and shook hands with the dean. "I appreciate your time in meeting with us," he said, and walked out the door. He was already in the hallway when Sarojini muttered her good-byes, embarrassed, smiling, but not looking at the history teacher.

Krishna followed his parents through the empty, darkened corridors that seemed so still and quiet. There was no hint of what happened here during the day; his parents had no indication of the clamor of his life: the petty alliances and friendships, the battle of egos, the cemented pecking order. He seemed above it all for a moment. Riding in the back of his father's Mercedes, past the grazing quarter horses under a gunmetal Kansas sky, he felt a strange sense of liberation.

ACKNOWLEDGMENTS

This book owes its existence to much more than the efforts of a lone author at her computer during late nights and early mornings at home, or during lunch at a day job. I would like to acknowledge the many people who encouraged me and helped make this collection a reality, and to thank:

My parents, Raghunath and Rekha Reddi, for making so many good things possible;

Chhaya Rao and Katherine Seidl, for believing when there was not much to believe in;

Members of the Cambridge Writers Group, past and present: William R. Crout, our fearless leader, Elizabeth Hatfield, Richard Harrison, the late Judy Johannet, Gregory Lalas, Ellen Litman, Jacqueline Malone, Elizabeth Morris, Joan Powell,

Mary Ellen Preusser, and Stephen Theodore, for many years of insight, patience, and literary companionship;

Anita Desai, for advising me to write with seriousness of purpose;

Daphne Kalotay, Julie Rold, and Mandy Smith, for reading, listening, and cheering me on;

Michael Mesure, Tara Ahmed, Esha Senchaudhuri, and Amy Onderdonk, for teaching me about birds, *bharatha natyam*, and veterinarian offices;

Lisa Starzyk, Patricia Giragosian, and my friends at the Boston Athenaeum, for providing me with "a room of my own";

The Vermont Studio Center, for their vote of confidence;

Anya Aleksiewicz Lownie, for lending me the eye of an artist;

Jennifer Crowe, for helping me find the time to finish;

Maria Massie, for being the dream literary agent I hoped for all those years;

Lee Boudreaux, for her editorial wisdom and unfailing good cheer.

About the author

About the book

Read on

P.S.

Insights,
Interviews
& More . . .

✳

Meet Rishi Reddi

© Debi Milligan

I WAS BORN IN HYDERABAD, INDIA, where the name Reddi (usually spelled with a "y") is very common. During my childhood, my parents frequently took me there on summer vacation. It was always an initial shock to me to see that name everywhere—on storefronts, in the telephone book, on dormitories on college campuses. It was such a contrast to how "different" I felt in the United States. Seeing the name posted on those signs made the city seem like home to me, but it wasn't really familiar at all.

As a young child, I moved with my parents to Great Britain, and then to the United States. We moved around a lot after we left India, because my father was very ambitious. He is a physician, and was very enthusiastic about the academic side

Please visit Rishi Reddi at www.rishireddi.net. If you would like her to participate in your book club via speakerphone, please e-mail requests to rishi@rishireddi.net.

of medicine, so we moved whenever he thought that a better position was available to him. We lived in quite a few cities, some very cosmopolitan, some not: London; Liverpool; Los Angeles; Philadelphia; Morgantown, West Virginia; St. Louis; and Wichita, Kansas. I spent a total of eight years in St. Louis and Wichita, so I consider myself to be most "from" the Midwest, but I found after moving to Boston that I was comfortable there, with its cosmopolitan population.

My parents thought that they would stay in the West for only a few years and then go back. They left India casually, as if on a youthful adventure, but like so many life paths, a chance decision became the history of their lives. But, whenever life was not going quite how they wanted, the decision to "go back home" always lingered as a safety net, a haven. I remember a couple of times when the threat—to me, it was a threat—of returning seemed quite real. But the decision was always made to stay. My parents would say it was because they did not want to disrupt my development and education but I also think that deep down inside they did not want to go back either. The longer that we were away, the more familiar the United States was compared to India, although they couldn't admit it. They'll probably be angry with me for saying that! ▶

> 66 We lived in quite a few cities, some very cosmopolitan, some not: London; Liverpool; Los Angeles; Philadelphia; Morgantown, West Virginia; St. Louis; and Wichita, Kansas. 99

Meet Rishi Reddi *(continued)*

I didn't have any brothers or sisters, and often felt uncomfortable socially. Books were a great relief to me. They were a fantasy world that I could escape to, a way to step into someone else's skin and walk around for a while (I think Atticus Finch says that in *To Kill a Mockingbird*). My reading was always greatly encouraged, especially by my mother, who used to read to me when I was quite young. Out of this love of books grew a desire to create one myself. I remember trying to write a book longhand when I was nine or ten years old. I never got farther than the first chapter, but the desire was there. In my senior year of college I took a creative writing class, and after I graduated, I articulated to my parents that I wanted to be a fiction writer.

My mother's family were elected officials and agriculturalists, and my father's family were doctors and engineers. They had no concept of what it would take, or mean, to be a writer. Although my mother had studied Telugu literature at the college level, the idea of making a living by writing was completely foreign to them. The struggle associated with it, and the expected meager financial payback, seemed crazy to people who had immigrated to a more technologically

66 I didn't have any brothers or sisters, and often felt uncomfortable socially. Books were a great relief to me. 99

sophisticated society in order to "make it big." My father advised me to become a professional, "stand on your own two feet" and then pursue the writing. I don't think he ever really expected me to follow through on the second part.

I wrote a few very lame stories before I went to law school, and sent them around to literary journals, but they never got anywhere—rightly so. In the meantime, I went to law school, got a job for the Massachusetts department of environmental protection and wrote in the mornings before I went to the office. The early morning was the time of day when I was at my most productive, and I spent it writing, not lawyering. I took some writing classes, and wrote some more. Slowly, some of my stories were accepted for publication. I enjoyed working as a lawyer; I liked the sense of working with a team to solve a problem, but I always was most enthusiastic about the writing.

The desire to commit myself to the writing was always there. When I was an undergrad at Swarthmore College, there was a rumor going around that James Michener, who was an alum, would hire people to help him with the background research for his books. After I graduated from law school, when my classmates ▶

> " The early morning was the time of day when I was at my most productive, and I spent it writing, not lawyering. "

were applying for real law jobs, I wrote letters and made a phone call to James Michener to see if he would hire me. I remember his assistant told me that there was no such job available—there never had been—but he commended me for my persistence.

I worked in the environmental legal field for ten years before I quit in order to finish *Karma and Other Stories*. When I left, I had been married for seven or eight months. I realized that if I was ever going to finish the collection, I had to do it then. It was the perfect opportunity: mooch off my wonderful new husband while we lived in a place with a mortgage that could be paid by one salary. I thought it would take me one year; it took me more than two . . . but he was supportive all the way. ✒

66 I worked in the environmental legal field for ten years before I quit in order to finish *Karma and Other Stories.* 99

The Indian Community I Knew . . . and the Indian Community I Never Had

MANY OF THE STORIES in *Karma* are set within the Massachusetts Indian American community. This was more by accident than by design; I lived in Boston when I started writing the stories and it seemed natural to set these imaginary people in a concrete place that I knew well. It helped me to write that way. I wrote the book over a period of almost ten years, and I started the oldest one, "Lakshmi and the Librarian," in 1996. The idea of having loosely linked stories grew over time, as I realized I wanted to set each story in the Boston area and that several of these characters would almost certainly know each other because they were part of the same immigrant Telugu community. It was important to me to write about Telugu-speaking people. Very few non-Indians that I knew in the United States had ever heard of the language.

During my childhood, my own sense of an Indian-American community was quite different from the one depicted in *Karma*. Because my family moved around so much, I missed that sense of belonging to a place. We moved to Wichita, Kansas, ▶

66 I wrote the book over a period of almost ten years, and I started the oldest one, 'Lakshmi and the Librarian,' in 1996. 99

when I was fourteen, and I remember being jealous of the children of my parents' friends who grew up in cities with large Indian populations like New York or Chicago. Before we moved to Kansas, I had taken Bharata Natyam lessons, but this stopped after the move because there was no dance teacher in Wichita. I was quite upset about not being able to continue the lessons; to me, they were a link with my Indian heritage, yet devoid of the tension between Eastern and Western behavior, and therefore a place of freedom. And the dance itself involves a beautiful sense of India's Hindu mythology—which I love—coming to life. When I moved to Boston for law school, I was surprised to learn that there were at least two well-established schools of Indian dance in the city. There is also a school called Shishu Bharathi, where Indian children meet on Sundays to study Indian culture and learn to read and write several of the regional Indian languages: Bengali, Gujurati, Kannada, Marathi, Punjabi, Sindhi, Tamil, and Telugu, as well as Hindi and Sanskrit. I took some courses there a few years ago to learn to write in Telugu—it was me and ten eight-year-olds sitting in a classroom at those little-kid desks. Subconsciously, I may

> **Subconsciously, I may have set these stories in Boston to create the Indian American community that I wish I had growing up.**

have set these stories in Boston to create the Indian American community that I wish I had growing up.

Many of the themes *Karma* addresses grew out of my family's own experience as immigrants in America. Writing it was a way for me to understand my parents' story, and thereby understand my own story. The intergenerational conflicts, the tension surrounding traditional gender roles, the differing views on sexuality, all of these occur among Indian immigrant communities regardless of geographic locale. Perhaps living in a location with a large Indian American population can mitigate the harshness of cultural adjustment—help a child feel "not so strange"—but it can't eliminate the shock altogether. Krishna, the protagonist in the last story, set in Wichita, would have had to struggle with the same issues no matter where he grew up. If he had lived in a town where he had more Indian friends, he could have had some support around resolving those issues, but he still would have confronted them.

My own childhood experience of Indian community was somewhat different than what is depicted in *Karma*. My family's Indian connections are spread across the United States, in many ▶

The Indian Community I Knew ... and the Indian Community I Never Had *(continued)*

different cities, and are centered in Hyderabad, where our ancestors have lived for generations. The Indian community that I knew growing up had immigrated to the United States at approximately the same time, did similar work, and were mostly part of the Reddy clan. The adults had known each other since they were children in Hyderabad or its surrounding rural villages, their own parents had been friends a generation before, and there was a lot of intermarrying. In America, they would call each other every Sunday to keep in touch, share gossip about what was happening in Hyderabad, and ask favors of people traveling back and forth from India: clothing to be brought here for a wedding, or medicine or gifts to be taken to family there. Our families would visit each other during the holidays, or we would take vacations together.

The sense of an extended family was quite palpable and the stories the adults told us kids of what happened during their childhood adventures had great charm. Our parents spoke to us of a different culture in an agricultural age, of people who had a great variety of spiritual, as well as superstitious beliefs. One of my uncles was a

66 Our parents spoke to us of a different culture in an agricultural age, of people who had a great variety of spiritual, as well as superstitious beliefs. 99

freedom fighter and had been jailed for his civil disobedience demanding that the Nizam's Hyderabad State join the Indian Union after independence. One of my grandfathers was a member of the first parliament that convened after the end of British rule. All of it was a great spark for my imagination. They were also describing a society in which, after the end of the British Raj, they were the most powerful members. They constituted the mainstream. That was totally foreign to me! I wondered if their stories could be wholly true. If India was such a wonderful place, if the moral values there were so superior, if the sense of family connection was so strong, why would they ever leave?

So I was intensely curious about India. The extended family vacations there, taken every other summer, were not enough to satisfy my curiosity. Because my parents were always with me, I felt I was always looking at the country through their eyes. I finally traveled there by myself in 1990 while I was a law student, and worked for an attorney who headed up the Lawyers' Collective, a nonprofit in Bombay. I was there for only four months, but it was an invaluable personal experience.

Things have changed much over the ▶

years. During the 1990s, there was a great influx of Indians who immigrated to the United States. Many have filled jobs in the IT sector, but there are also those working for low wages and a number of undocumented immigrants as well. The Indian American community is more economically diverse now. I'm currently active with SAALT (South Asian–Americans Leading Together), a national nonprofit group whose mission is to ensure the full and equal participation of South Asian–Americans in civic life in the United States, and to create a South Asian–American political identity. Such a group would have never existed even fifteen years ago.

When my family came to the United States in 1971, there were few people from India here, and the ones that immigrated were almost all extremely well-educated and had the potential for affluence: doctors, engineers, academics and scientists. There were few Indian food stores, restaurants, or Hindu temples. No one knew about Bollywood. In the grocery stores, people would approach my mother and speak to her in Spanish. There was very little knowledge of India, much less of Hyderabad and the language of Telugu. Of course, there was the hippie

> " I'm currently active with SAALT (South Asian–Americans Leading Together), a national nonprofit group whose mission is to ensure the full and equal participation of South Asian–Americans in civic life in the United States, and to create a South Asian–American political identity. "

movement, but it had reinterpreted Indian culture for its own purposes and didn't ring true with us. So, the difference between how my family lived and thought, and how my American friends and mainstream Americans lived and thought, made quite an impact on me. This is what I wanted to write about.

Author's Picks
Books That
Inspired *Karma*

HERE ARE SOME BOOKS that I enjoyed that I know were knockin' around in the back of my mind as I wrote these stories:

BELOVED by Toni Morrison

I love this book.

FAMILY MATTERS by Rohinton Mistry

Rohinton Mistry's novel about a Parsi family is so well-told and so authentic that I feel that, next time I'm in Bombay, I could knock on a particular door and see them all in their living room. After I finished the book, I found myself missing the characters.

FASTING FEASTING by Anita Desai

Anita Desai's novel of an Indian family that sends their treasured youngest child, a son, to the United States for college, is a moving depiction of what is emotionally unavailable in both societies. What's especially unnerving is her portrayal of how some children are more loved by parents than others, and how gender can play a role in that love.

> **What's especially unnerving [about *Fasting Feasting*] is [the author's] portrayal of how some children are more loved by parents than others, and how gender can play a role in that love.**

THE GOD OF SMALL THINGS by Arundhati Roy

This is a lyric, disturbing novel by Arundhati Roy set in Kerala, India, that addresses class differences and a family torn apart.

HUCKLEBERRY FINN by Mark Twain

When I read this book in high school I remembered thinking that I wanted to write like this someday . . . funny and serious all at once.

IF YOU WANT TO WRITE by Brenda Ueland

Written by the wise and irreverent Brenda Ueland in 1938, this is a book that I reread almost every year. I wish Brenda were alive now and would run for president.

INTERPRETER OF MALADIES by Jhumpa Lahiri

This beautiful collection of short stories describes the Indian American community in great depth of detail, and chronicles the lives of modern immigrants.

JOY LUCK CLUB by Amy Tan

This book, a favorite among so many readers, was among the first that I read that addresses family immigrant matters. Its depiction of mother-daughter relationships was especially moving to me.

Author's Picks *(continued)*

RUNNING IN THE FAMILY by Michael Ondaatje

Michael Ondaatje's fictionlike memoir showed me that family lore makes great material for good fiction. You can feel the warmth and sunshine of Sri Lanka in the pages of this book.

YOU ARE NOT A STRANGER HERE by Adam Haslett

I like all the stories in this very accomplished collection by Adam Haslett. I *love* the first story, written in the voice of a very likeable schizophrenic father.

66 Michael Ondaatje's fictionlike memoir showed me that family lore makes great material for good fiction. 99

Don't miss the next book by your favorite author. Sign up now for AuthorTracker by visiting www.AuthorTracker.com.